No
Holding
Back

No Holding Back

KATE EVANGELISTA

Sw♥♥n
Reads

SWOON READS | NEW YORK

A SWOON READS BOOK

An Imprint of Feiwel and Friends

Our books may be purchased in bulk for promotional, educational, or business use. Please contact your local bookseller or the Macmillan Corporate and Premium Sales Department at (800) 221-7945 ext. 5442 or by e-mail at MacmillanSpecialMarkets@macmillan.com.

Library of Congress Control Number: 2016936949.

ISBN 978-1-250-10062-7 (trade paperback) / ISBN 978-1-250-10063-4 (ebook)

Book design by Liz Dresner

First Edition—2016

10 9 8 7 6 5 4 3 2 1

swoonreads.com

For love . . .
Because it's too beautiful to be hidden in the closet.

For my whole life, we never crossed the line.
Only friends in my mind, but now I realize . . .
It was always you.

—MAROON 5, "IT WAS ALWAYS YOU"

Prologue

NATHAN PUSHED THROUGH the undergrowth into the Fort of Solitude, wondering how someone could run away from their own thirteenth birthday party. He and Preston had found the small clearing created by a circle of trees while playing a warped version of cops and robbers his cousin Caleb cooked up one summer, where the robbers actually escaped into the woods and the cops had to hunt them down. It was their special place—where they could escape when life wasn't particularly cooperative. Usually it was used for afternoon homework sessions and disappearing acts from pesky piano lessons.

Balancing a porcelain plate with a slice of the richest chocolate cake known to man in one hand—which should be considered a sin to eat, according to his mother—he used the other to shake out the leaves that hitched a ride on his hair and the cerulean cashmere sweater he'd bought specifically for the occasion. The color brought out his eyes. In fact, he'd gotten several compliments on it already.

Sitting against the trunk of the largest tree was the birthday boy. Beside him lay his discarded blazer. His sun-kissed blond hair tumbled over hooded eyes. With a stick he'd no doubt picked up along the way, he drew patterns on the ground. The other arm was neatly tucked into a sling as blue as Nathan's sweater. Beneath the crisp white shirt was a tight bandage around his shoulder to make sure he didn't further injure the rotator cuff he'd torn from overtraining a week ago.

On any normal day, the atmosphere at their hideout was light. Airy even. That day, a heavy black cloud hovered above Preston. It was as if the world had just ended, despite the celebration being held not a hundred yards away. Nathan picked up the heavy silver fork and swiped the tines through the inch-thick sugar icing that generously coated the slice he'd brought with him.

After a lick of sugary goodness, he grinned and said, "You know, it's not a birthday party when the birthday boy is out here sulking."

A snort was the response.

Okay, clearly Preston wasn't ready to explain himself; although Nathan had an idea where the sudden need to be alone had come from.

"Have you ever seen such a grand birthday party?" He glanced over his shoulder. Preston continued doodling on the ground, creating a collage of disturbed soil, scattered leaves, and a smattering of pebbles. Sighing, Nathan returned his gaze toward the Grant Estate. "I've decided. I'm going to be a party planner."

Another snort, then the words, "That's not a party."

Nathan turned around and faced the depressed mound. "What are you saying? It's brilliant! The food is delicious. Drinks are flowing like a river. And the decorations. Don't even get me started on the decorations. You have to give me the name of your mother's florist."

Finally Preston lifted his piercing green eyes and focused them on Nathan. The thin line of his lips quirked into a snarl as he said through his teeth, "It's stupid."

"Were you expecting a bouncy house, a magician, and a pony?" Nathan asked in a cooing tone.

"Go-karts," Preston grumbled.

"Can you really see your mother at a racetrack, handing out lemonade in red plastic cups?"

This time when Preston snorted, there was clear humor behind it. He dropped his gaze back to the forest-floor art he had been creating, but the motion of the stick didn't seem as deliberate as before.

Then he pointed the stick toward his house. "Anything is better than whatever the hell that is."

"Aren't you forgetting one important thing?" Nathan indicated his own shoulder with the fork he held.

Preston threw the stick away and ran the fingers of his free hand through his hair, making the perfectly combed strands stand in different directions. "Screw the party. I didn't want one anyway."

A soft smile stretched across Nathan's face. "Believe me, I'm on your side, but to be honest, I love all of it. Mark my words. I'm going to be planning parties even grander than this one. I'm even going to plan one for your mother."

"You know the guy who planned today actually broke down? Last I heard, he checked himself into a facility."

The warning only infused more determination into Nathan's declaration when he said, "Every knight needs a dragon to slay. You'll see."

Chuckles replaced the earlier snorts, and Preston covered them with a closed fist. Mission accomplished. The dark cloud above him looked more gray than black, slowly dissipating. Gone was the knot between his eyebrows. But almost immediately a groan stifled the laughter.

Heart in his throat, Nathan rushed to his friend's side. His hand hovered over Preston's uninjured shoulder.

Afraid to touch him for fear of causing more pain, Nathan asked, "What can I do?"

Preston grabbed his bound shoulder and breathed, each inhalation coming in deep and fast. A light sweat coated his forehead—agony clear on every line of his pale face.

"Come on," Nathan urged. Seeing usually tanned skin ashen was a cause for great alarm. "We need to get you to the hospital."

"I'm fine." Preston resettled his back against the tree, eyes closing.

"You don't look fine."

"Leave it alone, Nate. I said I'm fine."

"What if you tore something again?"

A tired laugh escaped Preston's lips, confusing Nathan enough to sit down, plate still in hand. In the distance, strains of Chopin from a string quartet hired for the event floated toward them, breaking the uncomfortable silence that followed.

"There's nothing left to tear," Preston finally whispered, color returning to his cheeks. "There's nothing left."

"I don't understand."

"I'm quitting swimming."

"No," Nathan said.

"There's no point—"

"No!" he cut Preston off. "You are not throwing away years of training just because of a rotator cuff injury."

"Fuck that. People quit all the time."

"Quitters don't succeed. And what kind of friend would I be if I supported every stupid idea that came into your head?"

"But—"

Nathan put on his I-don't-give-a-fuck face, interrupting Preston again. "Aren't you being way too overdramatic about this?"

"You know! If I didn't train, I wouldn't have gotten into that swimming camp."

"And are you in that swimming camp now?"

Preston swiped his free hand down his face. "Fu-uck! I hate this."

"With proper physical therapy, you will swim again. In fact, your shoulder will be stronger than ever, which can only be a good thing, considering we're aiming for Olympic gold here. I did the research."

"*We're* aiming?" Preston arched an eyebrow.

"I've taken it upon myself to see you fulfill your dreams, Preston Ulysses Grant."

"Oh?"

"Don't 'oh?' me like I'm joking! I will personally search for the best physical therapists in the country—"

"I think my parents have that covered."

"And I will be at every session," Nathan continued, as if his friend hadn't spoken. "You are going to heal, and you are getting back into the pool. I promise you that, or my name is not Nathan Parker—"

"Future party planner extraordinaire."

"You're catching on." Nathan picked up his fork again and helped himself to a bite from the slice lying on its side.

But before he could bring the piece to his mouth, Preston stole the fork.

"Hey! No fair. Get your own cake!" Nathan protested, but the bite was long gone.

Levering himself up onto his knees, Preston stabbed the slice and pushed almost half of it into his wide-open mouth, causing a rain of crumbs and icing down his front.

In order to keep from ruining his own clothes, Nathan fell back in disgust.

"Good thing you came," Preston said, happily chewing. "I thought I was going to starve to death out here."

One

NATHAN WAS RIGHT where he wanted to be—hands clasped and biting down on the tips of his thumbs in a futile attempt at settling the tendrils of nerves coiling in his stomach. Maybe at the moment it didn't seem like he wanted to be where he was, considering his legs bobbed as he sat among the multitude of family and friends cheering on loved ones currently competing for a coveted spot in the Bennett Club. But yes, he was right where he *needed* to be—aging ten years in a matter of minutes. He wouldn't be surprised if he walked out of that facility with gray at his temples. God forbid.

The prestigious, privately owned swimming club in Colorado that Preston was trying out for boasted of producing the best of the best. Any kid who dreamed of being a champion swimmer dreamed of being coached by Bobby Bennett. Banners suspended along the walls of the gigantic state-of-the-art facility featured twenty-foot pictures of past Olympians—medals and fists raised in triumph. They were undeniable proof of results.

His gaze slipped to the empty seat next to him, where his sister Natasha would have sat had she not made some lame excuse for not coming along. In fact, they all should have been there cheering Preston on. But Caleb had classes at Loyola he couldn't miss.

Nathan sighed. He could still remember the absolute determination on Preston's face when the invite had been delivered via special courier. The envelope came a couple of days after his cousin canceled their European adventure to sweep Didi—now his girlfriend—off her feet. Only about a hundred were given out every year. And only a handful of swimmers were actually chosen. It was akin to finding the golden ticket wrapped around a chocolate bar. Preston hadn't even finished reading the letter before he had dropped everything and started packing.

For years one of Nathan's favorite things to do—besides planning magnificent parties—was watch Preston swim. It was like watching performance art. The way his arms sliced through the water, each stroke pulling him forward with speed and precision. The way his back muscles flexed took Nathan's breath away every time. It must be the closest someone could get to the perfect balance between physicality, endurance, and concentration.

Well, maybe not right this instant, since the swimming god was completely botching things.

"What the hell are you doing?" Nathan yelled, jumping to his feet and shoving his fingers through his dark brown hair—a Parker trait he shared with his twin sister and cousin. If strands happened to separate from his scalp from pulling too hard, he didn't care.

His shoulders tensed when Preston finished third in the hundred-meter freestyle. He removed his goggles and swimming cap in one smooth pull. Panting, he looked up at the digital board displaying lap times.

Even from afar Nathan could feel the frustration radiating off his friend. To qualify for Team USA, a swimmer had to finish at least second in his respective event. Anything less was unacceptable.

Time for an ass-kicking.

To say Preston ate, slept, and breathed swimming was an understatement. It wasn't even a stretch to say he devoted every waking moment to the sport. As soon as he was old enough to figure out how to hold his breath underwater, he'd been a swimmer. He knew nothing else. Didn't want to do anything else. Watching Michael Phelps bring home seven gold medals in a single Olympics set his benchmark. His ultimate goal.

And what a complete loser he'd been all day.

Beyond frustrated, Preston slapped his hands on the pool's edge and heaved himself up. He hadn't always been this wobbly in the water. Coming in third? He couldn't even remember the last time that had happened. He should have been kicking their asses. There were only a few heats left. If he didn't make something happen soon, he could kiss joining Coach Bennett's team good-bye.

Sure, he might still be able to train elsewhere in preparation for the Olympic Trials in June next year, but it wouldn't be the same. Being part of the Bennett Club would give him the edge he needed. It was already the end of August. Many of the other private clubs were full, and he'd said no to all the collegiate team coaches for this, his best chance at becoming an Olympian—and he was sucking spectacularly. Maybe he should have kept his options open.

Fuck.

He snorted into the towel thrown at him by one of the staff. As far as he was concerned, Coach Bennett was it. The dream coach. If he couldn't make it into the Bennett Club, then what else was there for him?

Nothing.

"What the hell do you think you're doing?"

He lifted his face from the towel to stare into the blazing blue eyes of the one person unafraid to call him out on his shit. At five foot ten, Nathan was in full battle mode.

"I just can't seem to gain my stride," Preston said, irritation at himself leaking into his words.

"Of course not," Nathan said. "You're too in your head about this."

Preston slanted a glance over to the silver-haired man in a blue jacket watching the swimmers with a keen eye and a stern expression. "I thought maybe . . ."

The slap on his chest forced him to return his gaze to Nathan. In a lime-green sweater and white slacks, he stood out among the men and women strutting around in tight Speedos. Yet something about the confidence in his stance made him fit in anywhere.

"Don't think about Bennett. No one cares about him."

Um, maybe I do? Preston thought.

But maybe that was it? That he cared way too much?

"Nate—"

"No!" Nathan interrupted, wagging his finger. "I don't want to hear any more excuses from you. I'm fed up seeing you lose."

"But—"

Nathan crossed his arms and cocked his hip to the side, displaying his best I-don't-give-a-damn-what-other-people-think stare. "We did not fly all the way to Colorado just so you could choke at the very last second. Third? Seriously? When was the last time you placed third in any race?"

"Then what do you think I should do?" Preston asked, heat creeping into his tone.

Nathan rolled his eyes as if the answer was obvious. "Maybe calm the fuck down?"

It dawned on Preston all at once. "I'm a fucking idiot."

"Exactly! Stop thinking too much about Bennett and focus all your energy on swimming." This time the slap against his chest was one of reassurance. "It's what you're best at. Stick with the butterfly for now."

"But those aren't until later."

The butterfly was the most challenging stroke, so the fly heats were always slated for last. Competitive swimmers had to be proficient in all styles, but everyone had a favorite stroke. Preston just so happened to possess the shoulder strength and the arm span that made him lethal at the one he enjoyed most.

Nathan tilted his head. "Better for you to rest up. How many heats are there?"

Preston did the mental count. "There's the hundred-meter and the two-hundred-meter."

Nathan's eyes grew saucer wide, as if he suddenly understood something he might not have at the beginning. "The freestyle has six heats, while the butterfly usually only has two. Somehow you got it in your head that being in the water more will show Coach Bennett what you're made of."

The last part sounded more like a question, but Preston knew it wasn't. "Maybe."

"Pres, you are one of the best swimmers I know."

"I'm the only swimmer you know."

"You can't afford to suck any more than you already have," Nathan said. "You're making me look bad."

Preston kept his expression blank, but inside he was wincing. Maybe even dying a little. But not from the obvious joke at the end of Nathan's words. He knew just how much he was sucking. The truth hurt like a punch in the gut.

Showboating. That was what he had been doing. Sure, he could deny it all he wanted, but it didn't mean it wasn't the truth. He wanted to be top dog. Unfortunately, he'd bitten off more than he could chew. Damn it all to hell.

"Switch gears," Nathan continued. "Show Bennett and everyone in this building why I flew a thousand miles just to watch you swim."

The corner of Preston's eye twitched. "Of course you're making this about you."

"Hell yes, this is about me." Nathan shot him one of his better grins. The kind that hid nothing from the world. "Don't embarrass me out there, Pres. Show them what you're really made of."

Preston snorted.

Nathan's features softened. "You're too stiff. Remember, just have fun. I know this is your dream. I know it might feel like the world is over if you don't get onto this team, but if you don't have fun, then it wouldn't be worth it either way. Trust your training. Breathe and loosen up."

And just like that, Nathan turned Preston's humiliation into renewed purpose. His fingers closed tightly around the towel he'd been holding. He faced the fifty-meter pool currently filled with his competitors. Somewhere along the way he'd let his nerves get the better of him when he should have been concentrating on what he did best.

"The bastards won't know what hit them," he said, meaning every word.

"That's what I like to hear." Nathan turned on his heel. As a parting shot, while walking away with a strut like only he knew how, he said over his shoulder, "Give them hell, Pres. Give them hell."

Heart beating in his throat, Nathan excused his way back to his seat. The final heats of the day would begin any minute. Preston's expression after Nathan had left him was all too familiar—stone-cold stoic. It was the one he always wore when he was about to dominate in the pool. Nathan should be more confident that he'd done all he could in the motivation department, but looking at the competition made it hard.

A horn blared. Just a short burst, but it was enough to quiet the crowd's murmuring.

Through the speakers, someone announced the first heat for the hundred-meter butterfly. Nathan pushed to the edge of his seat. This was it.

The spectators came alive again as one by one the participating swimmers strode to their lanes. Whistles and cheers followed. When Preston appeared, Nathan's thundering heart all but stopped in his chest. Preston looked good. More relaxed. He had a sureness in his stride. That was the image Nathan always had of Preston—a force to be reckoned with. Calm. Collected. Ready to annihilate.

Once at their respective lanes, the competitors began stripping out of their warm-up jackets and pants down to their jammers. And damn if Preston, at six foot two, didn't look the best in them. They started at his hips and stopped above his knees. The way the cut of the material emphasized the V of muscle below his six-pack was enough to drive anyone insane. And that glorious perpetual tan he sported made him stand out. Nathan could stare all day and not get tired of what he was looking at.

Another short blast of the horn signaled the swimmers to get on their marks.

Preston stepped up onto the starting block. Like he always did, he rotated his shoulders forward, then back, followed by twisting his head left, then right. He bent his knees and flapped his arms until his hands slapped his shoulder blades. Then he touched his fingertips to the edge of the block. Patiently waiting, he faced forward with singular focus.

Nathan hadn't breathed since Preston took his position. Nothing could tear his gaze away from lane four until the race was over.

A hush spread across the bleachers. All eyes were glued to the pool with its bobbing red and yellow buoy lines that separated each lane. Anticipation crackled in the air, causing goose bumps to crawl up Nathan's arms. Again he clasped his hands together. This time it was for an entirely different reason.

A whistle blew.

Like a whip crack, Preston pushed off the block—the long line of his body arching through the air.

Two

WATER WAS PEACEFUL. Water was purpose. Water was all.

Preston found a sense of contentment and clarity when he swam. It was as if nothing could touch him. At the same time, water was his battlefield. His arms and legs transformed into lethal weapons, propelling him with a single-minded purpose. All his muscles were attuned to what his brain wanted, which was to win. To dominate. In a particularly fierce fight—like the one he was currently in—he focused on the only vital thing in that moment: breathing control.

It began with a sharp inhalation. A short hold that provided much-needed oxygen to his limbs. A quick exhale to expend the CO_2. And beginning again with another inhale as he crested the surface. A beautiful cycle that drove him until he reached the edge of the vast expanse fifty meters created.

At the end of the red five-meter marker, he tucked over and under until he faced the direction he had come from. He'd done it so many times during the course of his swimming career that he no longer had to think as his feet touched the opposite wall. Muscle memory kicked in and he was thrust forward—a speeding torpedo headed for home.

Why he'd insisted on swimming freestyle was totally beyond him. It shouldn't have taken Nathan coming down from the bleachers to remind him what he was the best at. The reason he had gotten the invitation to try out in front of the infamous Bobby Bennett in the first place was that he was a record-breaking butterfly champion, shattering statewide and countrywide lap times as if they were merely a suggestion.

With his height and arm length, fifty seconds was all he needed to finish a hundred-meter heat. His best time came at just over forty-nine, but he'd already been swimming all day. As long as he came in first, lap time mattered little at this stage.

He pushed all his regrets out of his mind and channeled his frustration into flying across the pool. Breathing through each stroke, he didn't worry about his competition. They all knew him by reputation. The swimming world wasn't all that big. And he would crush them. Without mercy.

In his periphery, the five-meter red buoys bobbed.

With each new breath he inhaled, he counted down. With the last rotation of his arms, he shifted all his strength to his legs for one final dolphin kick.

His palms made contact with tile.

Like a bullet out of a gun, relief shot through him. Pulling off his goggles and cap, his gaze scanned the digital board. He was a full two seconds ahead of second place. And most gratifying of all was his shattering of the current world record set in the last Olympics. He roared in triumph.

The swimmer in lane five slapped his shoulder, calling him a beast. He was beyond hearing anything else when he noticed Coach Bennett staring straight at him. It was like looking at the face of God. Certainly for swimmers.

That caught his attention, Preston thought.

Satisfied, and maybe a little too full of himself, he pushed out of the pool. With the number of swimmers participating that day, the organizers had to divide tryouts into several races. He would swim in another hundred-meter, then a couple of two-hundred-meter heats.

Regaining his confidence, Preston padded toward one of the showerheads lining the wall and rinsed off. Ten minutes until he would be back in the water.

In all the excitement, Nathan hadn't noticed his phone ringing until the crowd quieted down. He did a quick search and found Preston resting in the Jacuzzi, chatting up other swimmers. His heart lurched.

In his mind he could already imagine the attention Preston would get when his career took off. Could Nathan really stand aside while someone else captured Preston's heart? Nathan wasn't blind to the lustful stares Preston had been getting.

But in the movies, when a friend fell in love with a friend, it usually spelled the end of the friendship. The thought of having feelings for Preston beyond the platonic scared the Prada loafers off him. There were two points for potential disaster that he could see so far.

One: Nathan could find the courage to finally confess,

risking their friendship. What if Preston didn't feel the same way?

Two: If Nathan managed to keep his feelings to himself, there was a great chance he would lose Preston anyway. If he didn't speak up, there was no guarantee he ever would.

Again his phone rang, jarring him away from the impossible knot he found himself in. Lose-lose didn't even come close to describing his situation. *Ah, crap.*

Instead of answering the call right away, he eased out of the bleachers. There was no way he was talking to whoever it was from inside the facility. He might as well be at a rock concert for all the noise.

Too bad the call ended just as he stepped outside into the unseasonably chilly early autumn air. It was the kind of cold people got sick from. Biting. Relentless. Unforgiving. And it wasn't even the dead of winter yet.

As chills reached into his skin and rattled his bones, he found himself silently thanking the universe that he didn't live in Colorado. His body wasn't made for subzero temperatures. And he would rather die than wear a parka. Not flattering at all. Although Preston did look good in a knit beanie.

It was with that tantalizing image that he returned the video call. The face of a gorgeous blond popped onto the screen almost immediately.

"Hi, honey," she said cheerfully. "What's got you smiling like a loon?"

All the blood in his body seemed to rush to his head. "Mom!"

That was the last time he was making a call without checking caller ID first. Stella Clark-Parker was a perceptive woman in a petite package. Natasha was the spitting image of her, except with the signature Parker dark hair and blue eyes.

"I called because I thought you'd like to know that Eleanor will be hosting the Society of Dodge Cove Matrons luncheon this year," she said in that singsong voice of hers.

It was finally Preston's mother's turn. *Excellent*. Nathan's mind immediately clicked into party-planning mode. The DoCo Matrons luncheon was easily the biggest event of the year. To host it was a huge honor and an almost impossible undertaking. It was a big get for party planners. With all the matriarchs in attendance, the success of the event could put a planner's name on the map. This was it. This was Nathan's chance to make a career out of his dream. Time to slay his dragon.

"Has she met with planners already?" he asked, rubbing his lips.

"I hear the vetting begins tomorrow and will last all week. There's already a line despite Eleanor's reputation." His mother's eyes twinkled. "I know that look."

"Preston and I will be back in DoCo tomorrow. Can you get me a meeting with her the day after? That will give me enough time to prepare a proper proposal."

"I can definitely do that." Concern replaced her amusement. "But are you sure about this? I mean . . . you are just coming off planning Caleb's birthday."

"No time like the present to make a splash. Can you imagine what getting this event will mean for my future?"

"Of course. One recommendation from Eleanor can set you up for life. But there will always be parties to plan, hon."

Nathan's eyebrows came together. "I don't get where you're going with this."

"Just because Caleb decided not to take his gap year doesn't mean you can't take yours. It took you months to plan it. Why not go on the trip and come back refreshed and inspired?"

"Mom . . ." His heart softened at the earnest concern that settled on her beautiful face. He suddenly felt the urge to hug her. "I know where you're coming from. Honest. I just can't let this opportunity pass. I already have several ideas that I think she'll like."

"Are you sure—"

"I'm sure," he cut her off gently. "Plus, I need to be in DoCo for Preston. I get the feeling it'll be a rough month for him after today."

"How are the tryouts going?" she asked.

Nathan sent up a silent prayer of thanks that his mother didn't push the vacation issue further. "Oh, you know. It started off slow when Preston got it into his head that he had to swim freestyle."

"But fly is what he's best at."

"That's exactly what I told him!"

"And because of that he won, right?"

"Of course. He's resting up for the next heat now."

"Will you know the results today?"

"That's what I meant about a rough month ahead." He recalled what was written on the invite. "Today is for observation. Videos of the heats are recorded, and every swimmer's performance will be evaluated. It'll take them a while to comb through everything, so the soonest we can expect results is late September or early October."

"That's weeks away." She pouted, bringing a youthfulness to her features that seemed to make her glow from the inside out. "Preston's not going to sleep a wink the whole of September until those results are in." She clapped her hands together once. "Oh, I have the best idea ever!"

Chills of a different kind ran down his spine. "I'm suddenly afraid to ask."

"Take him to Europe."

"What?" He felt his throat tighten.

"We all know Preston has a tendency to obsess. That boy has nothing but swimming on the brain. You wouldn't want him to injure himself from overtraining again, would you?"

"Way to fight dirty, Mother." Yet Nathan couldn't stop the exasperated smile from forming on his lips.

Then she put on her serious-mom face, which never failed to make him chuckle. "This way you can take that vacation you obviously need and Preston is distracted from thinking about the results too much. It's a win-win in my book."

Nathan straightened to his full height and squared his shoulders. "I know you mean well, and I love you with all my heart, but I have to put the kibosh on your scheming. Preston isn't a little boy anymore. He knows better than to overtrain. And I will be there keeping an eye on him in between planning this luncheon."

"You really want this, don't you?"

He wasn't exactly sure what she meant, but he nodded anyway.

She tsked. "And to think, Europe is so romantic this time of year."

"Mom!" His cheeks burned like the pits of Hades.

"Did you really think you could hide it from me?"

He shook his head in defeat. "Is it too much to ask that I keep this to myself?"

"To be honest, I don't know why it took you this long to realize it. Just looking at the two of you, it's obvious."

"I don't know about that."

Her shining hazel eyes widened into perfect marbles. "Oh?"

"I don't think Preston feels the same way." There. He'd said it.

"Oh, honey," she chuckled, "he thinks about swimming and nothing else, so of course it will take him time to actually realize what his heart already knows. But if you take his focus away from the pool, I'm sure he'll catch up. Eventually."

As much as Nathan wanted to believe her, he couldn't bring himself to. "Life's not that easy, Mom."

"Of course not. But that doesn't mean you can't have fun while untangling the knots."

"I don't think I'm willing to sacrifice years of friendship for that."

"If Preston stops being your friend just because you love him, then he wasn't really your friend to begin with."

Instead of arguing with her, he smiled and said, "I love you."

Almost instantly after he uttered those words she teared up, placing a hand on her trembling lips. "Oh. Oh. I love you too, baby. To the moon and back . . ."

"And everything in between," he finished.

"Okay, go." She fanned her pink face. "I'm sure you'll want to see Preston kill it on the two-hundred-meter."

He blew her a kiss. "See you tomorrow. And, Mom?"

"Hmm?"

"Thank you for telling me about the luncheon."

"Anything for you, hon. But will you please consider the vacation? Take Preston, don't take Preston . . . just consider it."

"Sure." The white lie came out seamlessly.

As much as the idea of Europe with Preston tickled him, he had more important things to do. The last thing he needed was rest when his future career was on the line.

Three

TWO DAYS LATER, Nathan stepped out of his cherry-red roadster and faced the imposing expanse of the Grant Estate, aka the dragon's lair. One of the biggest homes in Dodge Cove, it housed one of its richest and most prominent families. He took a deep breath, forgetting for a moment that he too came from a lineage that had sailed the ocean on the *Mayflower*. That day he was a potential employee, and like any professional, he set his family name aside and reached for his tablet before he closed the door.

Running on two hours' sleep and every form of caffeine legal to ingest, he approached the gray stone mansion. He had spent all his time preparing at least ten different proposals for the luncheon. For anyone else, ten seemed excessive, but considering who he was pitching to, he wanted to be prepared. He was certainly the youngest party planner she had agreed to consider.

Sure, he had used his mother's friendship with Mrs. Grant to set up the meeting, but actually landing the gig was on his shoulders alone. Being her son's childhood friend wasn't enough. Despite her reputation for breaking the best of planners, he admired her standard for perfection. Nothing less would do. That was the vision and mission of the business Nathan dreamed of creating around the success of this event.

His finger shook slightly when he pressed the doorbell at the massive double front doors, with their lion statues at each side and snarling gargoyle knockers. Normally he would just walk in. He had certainly grown up at the Grant Estate as much as Preston had at the Parkers'. But that day he wanted to approach this meeting like the other planners invited.

A maid in a black dress and white half apron tied at the waist opened the door and greeted him with a subdued, "Good morning."

He smiled and said, "Nathan Parker here to see Eleanor Grant."

She stepped aside and opened the door farther, gesturing for him to enter. "She is in the sunroom."

"Thank you." He nodded once at her, then made his way across the white marble foyer, with its commanding sculpture of Atlas carrying a bronze version of the world on his shoulder.

As children, he, Preston, Caleb, and Natasha would play king of the hill, using the statue's other shoulder as the hill. It was a hoot until they got caught. He pushed away the loneliness that came with thoughts of their group. Things had changed so much that Nathan was terrified to rock the boat with his feelings for Preston.

Past the living room, down a long hallway where paintings

of several masters hung, was the sunroom. Voices in hushed argument brought Nathan's thoughts back to the present and what he was about to face. As he approached, he recognized Preston's deep tone quickly followed by his mother's clipped replies.

Unsure if he should just enter, Nathan paused by the door.

Two-thirds of the room's walls were made of glass, affording beautiful views of the meticulously curated gardens and fountains. Miniature orange and lemon trees sat in pots at every corner. Their fruits gave the air a refreshing citrus scent. Baskets with colorful flowering plants hung from the ceiling.

At the center of the rose-colored tiled floor was an elegant wrought-iron table with matching chairs. On one of them, teacup in hand, sat Eleanor Grant in an understated white Prada day dress paired with Gucci pumps and heirloom pearls. She had her blond hair, a shade lighter than her son's, in a tight twist at the back of her head. The harsh do accentuated the sharp angles of her features, giving her a hawkish beauty.

Beside her sat Preston. The feelings unearthed just by seeing him still blindsided Nathan. It was as if his heart leapt into his throat each and every time he caught sight of that cascade of blond hair, tanned skin, and broad shoulders. Preston's hair was still wet, hastily combed back. Even his shirt was damp in several places, like he'd rubbed a towel over his body without really thinking of drying himself thoroughly before getting dressed. The best evidence of all? An inch of black jammers peeked out of the bottom of his Bermuda shorts. The lack of a place setting in front of him was also suspect.

"I'm not sure," Preston said, a scowl forming as he crossed his arms.

Eleanor sipped her tea before responding. "We did not raise you to doubt your abilities."

"But coming in second at the two-hundred-meter fly?" Fingers raked into the tumble of sun-kissed waves. "That's unlike me."

"It cannot be helped. You had been swimming all day. Maybe you shouldn't have bet on swimming the freestyle."

Any other child would have cowered at the stringent tone. Not Preston. In fact, that was Mrs. Grant's normal speaking voice. She was much more severe when miffed. And the more annoyed she got, the quieter she became. If she was still speaking in long sentences, she was still in a placid mood.

"You sound like Nathan."

A corner of her eyebrow twitched. "Be glad that he was there to set you straight. I would have said worse if I were in his place. Sometimes I think that boy is too soft when it comes to handling you."

Nathan didn't know whether he should be insulted or flattered.

"I should have done better," Preston countered. "I know I could have done better." He pushed away from the table and began pacing. "Results aren't for a few weeks. I could have done more. I should have done more."

And there it was—the obsessing that Nathan was afraid of. Since leaving the facility, Preston had been unusually quiet. If Nathan hadn't been preoccupied with planning for this luncheon pitch, he would have caught the swimmer's worrying earlier. The pacing alone showed just how agitated he was. Preston wasn't a pacer. Not unless he was under tremendous self-imposed pressure.

"Will you sit down?" The venom in the question showed the limit of Mrs. Grant's patience.

Not good. Catching her in a bad mood would only hinder his chances of getting the job. Making a snap decision he prayed was for the best of everyone involved, Nathan knocked on the door frame.

Mother and son turned their stunning gazes toward him. He momentarily forgot what he had intended to say.

"Nathan, you're early."

The dragon's voice snapped him out of his stupor. After a quick throat clearing, he said to her, "Good morning, Mrs. Grant. I know I'm a little early. I hope you don't mind."

"I don't appreciate being caught unawares. That is why we set specific times to meet."

"I sincerely apologize, but I believe I have a solution to your problem."

"My problem?" The earlier eyebrow twitch turned into a full eyebrow arch. She gestured for him to come closer.

Gripping his tablet to keep from fidgeting beneath the sure gaze of the woman who held his future in her flawlessly manicured hand, he came closer until he stood behind one of the unoccupied chairs. He kept his gaze on her, blatantly ignoring the potent stare Preston treated him to. He was just as hawkish as his mother when he wanted to be. His still silence was clear evidence of it.

"Yes." Nathan kept his gaze on the prize, whose posture was nothing short of perfect. "It's clear that Preston needs a distraction."

"Nate," the topic of their conversation growled.

The heat in his voice told Nathan he was barely keeping the

curses in. Preston loved to cuss. But in the presence of his mother he had to keep the dirty words in or risk soapings of both the literal and emotional kinds.

"I'm listening." She picked up her teacup once again.

Steeling himself, Nathan continued. "As you may have heard, my cousin has opted out of his gap year."

"I must say I enjoyed that lovely birthday party you threw for Caleb," she said, returning the cup to its saucer without the expected *click* others doing the same thing would have made. "Roaring Twenties. Such opulence. Not my personal taste, but still impressive."

"Thank you." He acknowledged her words with a nod, striving for calm while his stomach performed somersaults. "As I was saying, I believe that it would do Preston some good to have something to think about other than the results. Shame to waste a trip that has already been planned."

"I can't go to Europe right now," Preston protested. "What if I'm called in for a retrial?"

His mother raised a fingertip and Preston immediately shut his mouth, but it was clear from the tightness of his shoulders that he had more he wanted to say. "Are you saying you are willing to take my son on this trip?"

"Only until the end of September or the results are announced, whichever comes first."

"But aren't you here to pitch for the luncheon?"

The question he had been waiting for almost brought him to his knees. He lifted his chin and went for the gamble. "Yes, I'm willing to give Preston the distraction he clearly needs, if . . ."

"If?" Mrs. Grant leveled a gimlet stare his way.

"Let me plan the luncheon."

"F—" Preston swallowed, cutting himself off.

His mother slanted a cutting glance over to her son. Even if he stood and she sat, it still seemed like she had the advantage of higher ground. "You are clearly on the brink of mentally breaking. According to the staff, you've been in the pool since dawn. Do you remember what happened the last time you focused too much on training?"

Preston reached up and squeezed his shoulder.

Nathan felt for him. As much as he wanted to round the table and stand by Preston's side as a show of support, he feared that if he moved, Mrs. Grant would refuse his proposal.

As if she read his thoughts, her stern gaze returned to him. "And how do you propose to plan the luncheon while running around Europe?"

Herein lay the risk of this harebrained plot. "I have all my contacts on speed dial. Many of the plans could be made over the phone and through e-mail. The luncheon isn't until the end of the first week of October. I can have everything ready for execution when I return. In fact, I have ten ideas for you to look at. Pick any one of them and I can move forward with the process."

"Ten proposals?" She folded her hands over her lap and regarded him with something close to an impressed expression. "The other planners only came with five at the most."

He cued up the presentations on his tablet and handed the device to her.

"You can't make me go," Preston said, reasserting his presence.

Nathan moved to stand by Mrs. Grant's shoulder as she swiped through the vision boards and panels that showed what he had in mind.

"Are you two seriously ignoring me?" came the indignant swimmer's question.

"How soon can you be in Europe?" she asked while still perusing the tablet's contents.

"We can be wheels up tonight if that would suit you," said Nathan, pointing at a table setting that he thought she would appreciate.

"Mother!" barked Preston. "I am an adult, and I can make my own decisions. I will stay if I want to."

Knot forming between her eyebrows, Mrs. Grant lifted her gaze from the tablet to spear her son with a commanding stare and said, "You should start packing."

Preston's face turned a purplish shade of red. He narrowed his gaze at Nathan.

"What do you think of the Rose Room as the venue?" Nathan asked, ignoring the daggers being thrown his way.

"Sounds promising, but at noon?" She glanced up at him. "The purpose of a luncheon is to actually have the meal at lunch. The Rose Room is more for high tea."

"There are many solutions around that. The roses would be in bloom. And against the backdrop of the fountain. Perfect."

Before she responded, she returned her attention to Preston, who was still glaring at Nathan. "You're still here."

"I don't need to go to Europe, Mother," he said.

To Nathan it seemed that each word was a curse aimed his way. He didn't mind. This was for Preston's own good. He wouldn't have suggested it otherwise. Planning the event would be so much easier if he was actually in DoCo for all the decision making. Couldn't Preston see what he was willing to sacrifice just to help?

"I'm sure that your father will agree with me."

Nathan's eyebrows lifted to his hairline. The dragon had brought out the big guns. Involving Preston's father was playing dirty. They all knew there was no refusing Arthur Grant. Especially when his son saw him as a man who'd hung the moon and stars.

From the way Preston opened and closed his mouth, Nathan's suspicions had been right. Seconds later, he stormed out of the sunroom, grim-faced, discreetly dropping several f-bombs along the way. Nathan wanted to laugh. He really did, but he was afraid of how Mrs. Grant would take it. Poor Preston. He would bitch the entire time but would thank Nathan for it in the end. He hoped.

Four

NOT ONLY HAD Preston's father agreed with his mother, but he'd even given Nathan access to the family jet for the duration. So Preston was committed to achieving his goal. What the fuck was wrong with that?

Sure, he'd overtrained in the past. He'd been an overeager idiot. Lesson learned. Which was why he couldn't understand why everyone seemed against him spending most of his time in the pool. He just needed to burn off the excess energy caused by having to wait for the results. That was all.

He knew what he was doing. The last thing he needed was an injury that might sideline him, or worse, render him unable to compete. But how could he say no to his father without seeming like a spoiled child whose toy had been taken away?

"Fuck this," he grumbled from across the aisle as the plane taxied down the runway in preparation for takeoff.

Nathan's fingers flew across the screen of his tablet. "You can do better than that."

"Fuck this shitty trip and you along with it," Preston revised, annoyed by the casual tone used to placate him.

"I get it."

"Admit it." Preston twisted around so he faced his kidnapper. "You're gloating on the inside."

Nathan let out an over-the-top sigh, which annoyed Preston even more. His friend was enjoying this a little too much. Acting casual on purpose. The traitor. Nathan knew how important this time was, and yet he was doing everything in his power to sabotage things. Preston should be home. He should be getting ready for the results—whenever the hell that would be.

Although . . . His performance had been so inconsistent. Crap one heat, then record-shattering the next. If he were Coach Bennett, he wouldn't accept him onto the team.

The thought almost crippled him.

"You know there are pools at the hotels." Nathan kept right on texting or e-mailing or whatever the hell it was he was doing as he spoke. "You can still swim your laps while we tour. No one said you had to stop training. This trip is just to keep you from obsessing over the results."

Too late.

Lips in a tight line, Preston slumped back into his seat as the pilot announced through the intercom system that they were about to take off, that they were expecting a smooth flight, and how many hours they would be in the air.

"Paris?" he asked, fishing out his phone. "Doesn't a European adventure typically start in London?"

"Yeah."

He saw Nathan shrug from his periphery as the plane picked up speed and the front end began tilting upward. With a smooth push and change in pressure, they were airborne. The lights of the airport and the city steadily grew smaller until they were pinpricks of illumination on the ground.

"Caleb and I already went to London," Nathan continued, most of his attention still on the screen. "I was thinking that maybe starting in Paris was the next best thing. Would you rather start in England? I can ask the pilot to change course."

Preston harrumphed as he waited for the pilot to inform them that it was all right to start using the onboard Wi-Fi. He hadn't checked his e-mail since they'd boarded. Maybe there was still time to turn this plane around.

"I'm here in protest," he said. "I don't give a flying shit where we go."

"Yeah, yeah, you're determined not to enjoy yourself. I get it."

Somewhere above the Atlantic, Nathan put down his tablet and looked out the window into the inky expanse outside. The red light at the tip of the plane's wing blinked rhythmically— slow, almost hypnotic. He'd had enough of e-mails from Eleanor for one day. Little did he know when he blurted out this scheme and became the luncheon's planner that she would immediately begin bombarding him with questions and suggestions.

He reminded himself that this was what he had wanted since he had figured out there were actual people who made it their business to plan parties. He knew what he was up against with Mrs. Grant. In fact, he'd spent years preparing for this moment. But it didn't mean he should be at her beck and call 24/7. The most important thing at the moment was his promise to get her son's mind off those damnable results.

It seemed Preston was already spiraling. The swimmer hadn't stopped looking at his phone since the pilot switched on the onboard Wi-Fi. Nathan glanced across the aisle.

From the way Preston's thumb kept tapping a specific area of the screen, he was pressing refresh over and over again. Nathan wanted to say something, but why bother? It would only annoy Preston more than he already was. Plus, there was nothing he could do while they were in the air. Might as well let him refresh to his heart's content.

When he and Caleb had started planning their trip, they'd focused on pubs and museums and many out-of-the-way sights that would enhance their experience of Europe. During that stage, Nathan had come across a local tourist attraction in Paris involving love locks. At the time he hadn't paid much attention to it, because why would he and Caleb want to go to a bridge for lovers?

But his mother's quip about Europe being romantic kept replaying in his mind as a slow blush crept to his cheeks. He rested his chin on the palm of his hand and returned to gazing out the window.

The scenario had become crystal clear to him as he purchased the lock from the hardware store. He would bring Preston to the bridge. There he would show him the lock with their initials on it and attach it to the railing. Then he would give Preston the key and tell him how he felt. That if Preston felt the same, he should throw the key away. It would be perfect. Assuming Preston threw the key.

After answering yet another e-mail, Nathan decided maybe it didn't matter if the person he cared for the most in the entire world didn't feel the same way. He just couldn't stand Preston not knowing. Would it change their friendship forever? Maybe. But Nathan wouldn't allow them to go their separate ways without saying anything. He would definitely regret losing that chance.

The worst-case scenario? Preston would reject him. Sure, he would be heartbroken and possibly lose his best friend forever, but it would also allow him to move on. At least, that was what he'd told himself when the idea for this trip had come to mind. Hopefully he wasn't just deluding himself, because maybe he wouldn't be able to handle the loss of Preston any better than Tash had handled the loss of Jackson.

Thinking of what had happened to his sister when that jerk left chilled his blood. Tash had practically burned DoCo down in her grief. But if Nathan didn't make his move, he might end up losing Preston anyway.

The best-case scenario seemed so far out there that it lived in another universe. Preston feeling the same way? Actually returning his feelings? Even the slightest hint of it tightened his chest to the point of pain. Not once had Nathan suspected anything. Although, in truth, besides being obsessed with the yummy front man of Maroon 5—because why not? Adam Levine was sexy as hell—Nathan hadn't really found himself attracted to anyone else. He'd dated, sure. But nothing stuck. And over the years he hadn't really seen Preston consider the idea of dating anyone. Well, he could easily attribute that to swimming. The guy did devote his entire being to the sport.

Either way, they both needed time away. Time to decompress. Time to enjoy themselves before they returned to reality. Preston would definitely get into the Bennett Club and eventually swim his way to Olympic gold. Nathan was sure of it to the marrow of his bones. While he would return to Dodge Cove and build his party-planning empire.

A couple of hours after landing, the bellman inserted the keycard into the slot of the two-bedroom suite Nathan had booked. The man opened the door and pushed the cart with their luggage inside.

His eyes on his phone, Preston followed, mind still on the acceptance e-mail. Or lack thereof.

"You really should be careful," Nathan said.

Preston felt a tug on his shirt from behind. Stopping in his tracks, he lifted his head and realized he had been about to collide with a potted ficus in the open living area that separated the bedrooms. Nathan rolled his eyes as he walked past, thanked the bellman in French, and handed him several Euros. Then he placed his phone and tablet on the desk by the balcony doors.

Preston sidestepped the plant and dropped onto the couch like a sack of potatoes. "How hard is it to send one e-mail?"

Hands on his hips, Nathan huffed, "It's only been a few days since tryouts ended. And quite frankly, I'm tired of this."

"Tired of what?" Preston asked absentmindedly, his attention back on the screen.

The phone was snatched out of his grasp.

"Hey!" He turned toward Nathan in surprise and made a grab for the device.

When Nathan didn't make a move to return it, Preston

blinked, unsure of what to do next. There was a purpose to this, and an explanation was forthcoming. Over the years he'd gotten good at waiting.

It didn't take long for Nathan to say, "I will return this to you if you tell me you haven't been checking for an e-mail from Coach Bennett since we left DoCo."

"Give it back."

"Then consider this phone confiscated."

Preston closed his hand around Nathan's wrist and pulled him down onto the couch. He shifted so he was on top. Nathan wiggled and squirmed, keeping the phone out of reach. Using his knees on either side of Nathan's hips, Preston pinned him in place. A sharp gasp caught his attention. He looked down to make sure he wasn't hurting Nathan, only to see the other boy staring up in amazement at him. Like he'd done something completely shocking.

Uncertainty washed over Preston. What had he done?

Meanwhile, the pause between them stretched on.

This was fucking stupid.

No longer willing to go along with whatever game Nathan was playing, Preston pushed off the couch and glared.

"Give me back the fucking phone!" He reached out, palm up.

Nathan sat up. "I know you're pissed, but hear me out."

"Just shut up and give me the goddamn phone."

"No."

In seconds it seemed all the blood rose to his head. In two steps he grabbed Nathan's phone off the desk.

"What are you doing?" Nathan got to his feet.

"You want my phone?" Preston tilted his head, still glaring. "Then I'm keeping yours."

"You can't—"

"Hypocrite," Preston cut him off.

"What did you say?"

"You heard me."

"Seriously, Pres, will it hurt you to be away from your phone for the rest of the trip?"

"Don't act like I'm the only one glued to my phone."

"I'm just trying to help get your mind off the results. It's clear you're already obsessing over them."

"I call bullshit."

"Oh yeah?" Nathan waved the phone in the air. "You've been pressing the refresh button since we left Dodge Cove."

A stillness came over Preston. "And who's been answering e-mails from my mother at the same time?"

"You know I've wanted this since we were kids. Your mother's recommendation would mean a step in the right direction for the business I want to build." Heat finally colored Nathan's tone. "Can't you see how much I'm sacrificing just to be on this trip with you while planning the luncheon remotely?"

"Sacrificing?" Preston threw his hands up. "What a load of crap! I never volunteered for this trip, but I'm here. Don't put this on me."

Before Nathan could open his mouth to rebut, Preston charged him. Surprised, he put his hands up as if expecting a blow. Preston took advantage of the opening and grabbed his phone out of Nathan's hand and shoved the other phone into Nathan's chest. Scrabbling, Nathan barely caught the device before it fell to the ground.

Preston headed for the door, no longer interested in continuing the fight. "I'll be in the pool."

"Pres . . ."

His hand paused at the knob. Without looking back, he said, "If you try taking my phone again, I'm going home."

The threat in his quiet words hung between them before he left the room.

Five

ROOTED TO THE spot where Preston had left him, Nathan had stared at the closed suite door for such a long time that a prickling had begun along his legs. He would have loved to stand longer, because his brain refused to give the command to stay put, and dropping to the floor seemed overly dramatic. Even for him. So, muscles like rubber, he hobbled his way to the couch.

"Preston, you idiot," he mumbled.

The moment his butt hit the cushion, he let out a long sigh. When he'd thought of taking Preston's phone, it was with the best of intentions. He had wanted to tease the gloomy swimmer into smiling. Maybe even coax out a laugh or two. The e-mail wouldn't come this early anyway. Pres was just too blind to see it. The invite clearly stated *end of September*. He doubted Coach

Bennett would make hasty decisions based on a person's swimming talent alone.

Not in a million years had he thought Preston would blow up in his face like that. The guy had a temper, sure, but at least he usually had a long fuse. Nathan had been called many things growing up. And he'd been in fights far worse with Preston. But never had he been called a hypocrite. That hurt more than any expletive. He *had* to work throughout the trip. It was a condition for taking Preston away in the first place. He had had a feeling Preston would be pissed, but he'd never expected that taking the phone—or attempting to take it—would turn nasty. It was a huge slap in the face.

And that threat at the end? What the hell was that about? Was Preston in that much stress that he would end this trip just for a phone? Insane.

Mind reeling, Nathan's hand ran up his thigh until his palm grazed the lock in his pocket. He had intended to convince Preston to take a walk to the Pont des Arts, which was a couple of blocks away from their hotel.

Doubt clouded the once-magical moment Nathan had carefully constructed in his mind on the plane ride over. Was he doing the right thing? Would things get worse? Would Preston think Nathan was making fun of him? That this was all a big joke?

Cold sweat dotted his brow despite the temperature control in the room. He scrambled for his phone and dialed the number of the one person who could give him much-needed perspective. Not even twenty-four hours in and already things were falling apart.

The phone rang and rang. And rang. He had engaged video

call, so instead of having the receiver against his ear, he stared directly into the phone's screen. When the call ended without being picked up, he checked the time. It was early evening in DoCo, so it would be impossible for Tash to be asleep.

He tried again. His knee bobbed like a bouncing ball.

Again the call ended. Could Tash be busy? It wasn't like his sister to ignore his calls. Even if it was the middle of the night, she would pick up.

Anxiety over the fight turned into worry for his sister. He tried one more time. If it didn't go through, he'd call their mother. Hopefully it wouldn't get to that point, because she was a worrier. Maybe Tash had her phone on vibrate or something.

On the fifth ring of his third try, Tash finally answered, but she had disabled the video call. Surprised, Nathan quickly brought the receiver to his ear.

"Tash?" he whispered around the knot in his throat.

"Nate," came the absentminded reply.

He sat up straight. "What happened?"

"It's nothing," she said quickly. "Why'd you call?"

His free hand balled into a tight fist. "Have you been reading the gossip sites again?"

After a brief pause, she said, "Stupid clickbait. I wasn't really seeking him out or anything—"

"But you know what happens when you go down that rabbit hole." He imagined her sitting alone in front of her computer, just staring at the screen.

"Hey! I'm not bawling my eyes out right now, am I?"

"Then why didn't you answer my call right away?"

"For all you know I could have been in the shower."

Nathan waited, unwilling to swallow the lie she was clearly feeding him. Clickbait or not, once she started down that road, it took her time to veer off.

"No one is supposed to meet their soul mate at five years old," she finally said after what seemed like an eternity. "We'd been together for so long I guess I just don't know anything else. We never even officially broke up."

Okay, that he wasn't expecting. But it certainly sounded like the truth. "Say again?"

"We grew up together. We experienced all our firsts together. He told me he loved me." She sighed. "He told me that he would always be there for me. That he would always be my forever. That he would go to the ends of the earth for me. And then he left."

This was an old story, told over and over again so that it almost sounded like a cautionary tale mothers told young children during the age of fairy tales and magic and dragons.

The princess fell in love with the prince. They were to live happily ever after. At least that was what the entire kingdom thought. Then the prince decided to leave, telling no one of his plans. The princess had no answers for what could have driven him away. Until one day news started spreading about the prince gaining popularity. That he traveled the world making music, and he had a different woman on his arm almost every night. The princess was inconsolable. And the world burned in her wake. The end.

"Why do you keep doing this to yourself?" he asked.

Like a wicked witch casting a spell, Natasha said, "Be careful. Love is like acid in the veins. It eats you from the inside out until there is nothing left."

Nathan grimaced, hating that his twin seemed to possess the ability to read his mind despite being in a crazy emotional state. "Cynical much? I think Caleb is rubbing off on you."

She laughed. "Not anymore. Our boy is happy."

"Please tell me you didn't give him the same 'Love Is Like Acid' speech."

"Of course not. It's too late for him. You, on the other hand . . ."

"Not every guy is like Jackson, you know," he said carefully, steering the conversation away from himself.

A loaded silence passed between them. At one point, he had to look at the screen just to make sure the call hadn't been cut.

Afraid that he had said the wrong thing, he qualified with, "What he did . . . The least he could have done was tell us. I honestly thought our friendship meant more than just abandoning us for a chance to travel the world as a DJ. We didn't even know he was into that sort of stuff."

"He was the one, you know," she said in such a small voice that all Nathan wanted to do was reach through the phone and hug her. Alas, the limitations of technology.

"Europe is looking pretty far right now. I'm sorry I can't be there."

"Nah."

Nathan had a feeling she was shaking her head. He really wished she hadn't disabled the video call.

"I'm being stupid."

"You're being normal."

"Ha."

He bit his lower lip before he said, "Please tell me you're staying home tonight."

"I'm good. Don't worry."

Would Preston pull the same stunt? Just up and leave? Just like he had threatened a few minutes ago? And when he'd become popular, which he would because he was delicious, would he flit from one person to the next until he eventually found someone who would steal him away forever?

The indoor pool was empty. Preston thanked his lucky stars. He couldn't deal with people. Not so soon after a blowup with Nathan.

So, lap after lap he swam. His arms sliced through the water like a warm knife through butter. Being in the water centered him enough to realize he had been harsh. Most likely, Nathan had reasons for wanting to take his phone. Of course, at the time, the panic caused by losing the potential link to his future had blinded him.

After he reached a hundred he pulled off his goggles and cap and thumped his forehead against the cool tile. He had been a monumental jerk, judging from the hurt and shock he had seen on Nathan's face. The last time he had lost his shit that bad had been during his physical therapy days. The pain of regaining movement in his shoulder coupled with Nathan being overly enthusiastic about his recovery had made him snap on more than one occasion.

"Ah, fuck," he muttered into the water before heaving himself out of the pool.

After showering and getting dressed, he padded back to their suite feeling more like the man his mother had raised. Being on a plane for hours had knotted him up badly. With his shoulders loose, he could apologize.

He slipped the keycard into the slot and pushed the door open the second the light went from red to green. Once he was inside, Nathan's voice reached him right away. It seemed he was talking to someone.

A grin pulled at the corners of Preston's lips. From the stress clinging to his friend's voice, he knew who Nathan was talking to. He entered the living room and found Nathan pacing the length of the balcony, which overlooked the Eiffel Tower in the distance. The sky was clear. The sun was out. They had arrived just before lunch. Shame to waste all that cooped up in their hotel room.

Crossing his arms, he leaned against the wall. Nathan rubbed his forehead with the thumb and forefinger of his free hand. He spoke rapidly into the phone. Then he paused, in both speaking and pacing. This must be Preston's mother grilling him about the plans for her party. Not twenty-four hours out of Dodge Cove and already Nathan's shoulders drooped. Would he survive?

Preston banished the question as soon as he thought of it. If there was anyone who could survive his mother and come out intact on the other side, it was Nathan. Preston had faith in his friend. Party planning was to Nathan as swimming was to him. He should have seen that earlier—during the phone-taking incident.

"All right," Nathan said, pulling Preston away from his brooding. "You can gloat."

It took him a second to realize the call had ended and that he was the one being spoken to. He blinked. "About what?"

Nathan wagged the phone in his hand.

"Ah." His own phone was tucked safely inside his pocket. Still no e-mail.

"Well . . . let me have it."

"Tempting." Preston pushed off the wall. "Considering you were just talking to my mom, I think I'll let you off the hook."

"She was wondering if she could change the tiles in the Rose Room. The tiles! Which have been there for over a hundred years." Nathan wilted into one of the wrought-iron chairs on the balcony. "No offense, but your mother . . . she's in a league of her own."

Preston threw his head back and laughed, a genuine sound that came from his belly. He'd been so tense about the godforsaken trip that he'd almost forgotten how to be amused.

"I'm so glad you're in a better mood," Nathan said in response.

"I have an idea." Preston fished out his phone and placed it on the coffee table between the two couches. "Let's leave these here and find a place to eat. I'm starving."

Like sunlight piercing through storm clouds, Nathan's face lit up. "That's the best offer I've gotten all day. Let's go."

Six

LUNCH WENT WELL, considering Preston's previous mood. When he ordered practically everything on the menu at the café they had chosen, Nathan knew all was right in the world. The fight, forgotten. Especially after the ravenous swimmer tried to steal a bite of Nathan's quiche, which he valiantly defended.

They had always been that way. Heated words meant nothing stacked up against years of loyalty and trust. Add to that the fact that Preston had calmed down significantly after a session in the pool. Expending excess energy always did him good.

Moods lighter from the hearty combination of carbs and excessive amounts of cheese, Nathan suggested they take a walk around the city to burn off some of the calories.

The pleasant and calming scent of baking bread seemed to waft straight from the bakeries into the air. It mixed with the delicious aroma of roasted chicken slathered in the most decadent butter. Both intermingled with the lingering acrid, musty fog of cigarette smoke. And underneath it all was the pungent odor of piss. Nathan breathed in deeply, banishing a case of nerves that knotted his insides.

This was his chance. What had he been afraid of, anyway? One fight meant nothing in the grand scheme of their lives. And that thing Natasha had said about love being acid? It was her way of looking out for him. It didn't mean he should turn away from confessing how he felt.

He moved his gaze toward the swimmer ambling along next to him and said, "When Caleb and I started planning this trip, I came across this really interesting bit about love locks."

Preston made a thoughtful noise as he stuffed his hands into his pockets.

Taking the gesture as a sign, Nathan continued, "You see, couples etch their initials on the face of the lock. Then they attach the lock to the railing of a bridge for the entire world to see. Isn't that romantic?"

No response. Preston kept walking, face forward.

"Anyway," Nathan said in his most cheerful voice, "throwing the key is said to be the ultimate symbol of forever, because the lock can never be opened ever again."

On and on he spoke, telling stories he had read on the Internet about couples who had traveled to Paris from all over the world just to attach a lock. Some of them had even used their life savings for a once-in-a-lifetime opportunity to show their love for each other. Nathan practically swooned on the spot, he was so caught up.

After about a block, it finally dawned on him how one-sided the conversation had become. He stopped. When Preston didn't stop along with him and actually made it a few yards without noticing anything, anger replaced the nerves in Nathan's belly.

Preston finally turned around with a look of utter confusion on his face, as if to ask what the hell Nathan was doing just standing there. As if it had been Nathan's fault that they were not walking anymore.

"You're not even listening to me." Nathan charged him and slapped his friend's chest with both hands. A double high five it was not.

"Hey!" Preston took a step back. Not that the impact had hurt. Nathan knew the swimmer could take more punishment than a couple of palms on his pecs. "What's with the violence?"

"See!" Nathan poked him. "That's the problem with you."

"Whoa!" Preston raised both his hands. "Where the hell is this coming from?"

"I'm so tempted to tell you to figure it out, but I know you have to be in the pool to do that."

What once was calm confusion turned into mild annoyance in those sharp green eyes. "What the hell are you talking about? I thought we were walking?"

"Duh! We *were* walking."

"So why'd we stop?"

"Because you're not listening to me." All the hurt from their earlier fight came rushing back. "That's the problem with you. If it doesn't have anything to do with swimming, you tune it out as if it's not important."

The snort that followed brought Nathan's rising anger up a couple of notches. Wary glances were tossed their way from people passing by, tourists and locals alike. He didn't care. Let them look.

"That's why I wanted to take your phone," he spat out.

Preston rolled his eyes. "Are we back to that? I thought I made it clear that I need my phone as much as you need yours."

"Yeah, and you called me—"

"Look"—Preston scratched the back of his head—"I don't want to fight about this anymore. I'm sorry for calling you a hypocrite. I'm sorry for zoning out. I was just thinking about needing to hit the gym when we get back to the hotel."

"Is that what this whole trip is going to be about?" Nathan's stomach fell, deflating some of his previous excitement. "All you're going to think about is the pool, the gym, and when that stupid e-mail is going to come?"

"It's not a stupid . . ." Preston let out another breath. Nathan could see that his friend was trying really hard not to engage in the fight, which knocked some of the wind out of his sails. "Just tell me what you were talking about and I promise I'll catch up."

That did it. No use fighting anymore. Preston made the face that never failed to soften Nathan's heart. The same lost look he had while hiding at their Fort of Solitude during his thirteenth birthday party.

Nathan's shoulders drooped as he said, "I was talking about love locks and how romantic it is that people go out of their way to express their love for someone special."

"That's complete bullshit," came Preston's immediate response. "Imagine what people could do with the time they spend on that kind of crap."

"Crap?" This time Nathan's stomach fell for a whole different reason. He had to force himself to speak around the hard lump that had formed inside his throat. "You think a romantic expression of love is crap?" His heart joined his stomach in the bottomless pit. "I seriously can't believe this. Caleb I would understand, because he once avoided love like the plague. But from you? I thought you were better than that."

"It's just locks. The tradition didn't even start in Paris."

"Just locks?" Nathan's head whipped up to pin Preston with a withering stare. "Just locks! They aren't just locks! They mean something to all the lovers who placed their initials on them and threw away the keys so their love would remain true forever."

"I don't understand why you're so upset. If you want, we can fly to Serbia and visit the Ljubavi Bridge, where this thing really started."

"I don't appreciate you patronizing me, Preston Ulysses Grant."

Preston shoved his fingers into his hair. "I'm not patronizing you. I just don't understand why you're upset over something so trivial."

The hurt caused by Preston's callousness poisoned all the hopes Nathan had for a confession. Was this really what his friend thought about love? That it was trivial? Nathan knew that Preston didn't go on a lot of dates, but he never seemed the type to be so cavalier. It scared Nathan to think of what his friend's reaction would have been if he had succeeded in telling Preston how he felt.

"I can't do this," he whispered, taking a step back.

"What—"

A head shake cut Preston off. Nathan took another step

back. The space he created between them felt like a great chasm. He couldn't help but wonder if that divide had always been there and he had been too blind to see it.

"Nate?"

Nathan raised a hand to stop Preston from moving forward. "I just want to walk around. Shake off this funk. I'll be fine."

"All right, let's go." Preston inclined his head toward the opposite bank. "Want to walk around the Louvre? I know you like looking at the *Mona Lisa* and telling me how fake her smile is. What do you say? Ready to criticize her until a tourist cries?"

Nathan's refusal came so fast that Preston was momentarily shocked by it.

"But you like art. You always drag me to the DoCo Museum every time they have a new exhibit on display."

"Maybe tomorrow," he said, not sounding like himself anymore.

"Okay. Uh . . . so what do you want to do now? Go back to our hotel? Or we can get that perfume your mom—"

"I just want to be alone right now."

"Nate, come on." Preston closed the gap between them but kept his hands to himself.

"Don't . . ." Nathan hugged himself and began taking several more steps back. "I'll meet you back at the hotel, okay? You can go to the gym. You're probably itching for a run on the treadmill. I shouldn't have suggested sightseeing after lunch."

"Nathan."

"Just leave me alone for a bit, Pres. I promise I'll be fine."

Still skeptical, Preston said, "All right."

Without a word of good-bye, he turned around and headed back the way they had come. Nathan's heart broke while staring at the back of the guy who he'd thought he knew from the inside out.

Goes to show. No one really knew everything about anyone. Years of friendship didn't guarantee that.

Swiping at a stray tear, Nathan kept walking in the direction they'd been headed. For the first time, he admitted to himself that maybe this trip hadn't been such a great idea. He passed bridge after bridge that connected the right bank with the left. There were thirty-nine in total, if he remembered the article he had read correctly.

When he reached the Pont des Arts, he stopped. A sign with a picture of a lock encircled and crossed out was planted at the entrance to the bridge.

"Where are the locks?" he asked no one in particular, voice small.

A couple dressed all in black who had been passing by paused in front of him, obscuring his view.

Having heard his question, the woman said in French, "The locks have been removed because they were making the bridge railing collapse." She glanced at the man in a long trench coat beside her.

He shrugged and said, "If you ask me, good riddance. Those locks were an eyesore. They finished replacing the old railing with some kind of material where nothing can be attached. They are doing the same thing with all the other bridges."

The couple spoke so fast that Nathan almost wasn't able to catch everything they were saying. Their cadence threw out words like bullets from a machine gun.

"Since when?" he finally found the courage to ask in French.

The woman exchanged a few words with the man, then said, "I believe they completed this yesterday."

"So if I'd only arrived days earlier . . . ," he said, his gaze dropping to the ground, spotting a glob of used gum on the cobblestones.

"Actually, no," the man said. "They have banned the attachment of locks for over a month now."

Unable to help himself, Nathan started laughing, then covered his face with both hands.

Great, just great.

Seven

AN HOUR ON the treadmill hadn't given Preston the clarity he had needed to understand what the hell was going on. What had Nathan been babbling about? Love locks? There were so many other things to do in Paris than attaching a stupid lock on a bridge. But the hurt on his face had been unmistakable. It had left Preston thinking he had done something stupid . . . again. Exactly what, he couldn't be sure.

Seeing as working up a sweat wasn't working, he returned to their hotel room and picked up his phone. Maybe another form of distraction would clear his mind. A quick e-mail check told him what he already knew. No response. Would there ever be one?

A call interrupted his thoughts. He grinned at the name that popped up and swiped his thumb over the screen. Stepping out onto the balcony, he brought the receiver to his ear.

"Is it that time of the month again?" he asked, not bothering with greetings.

"Shouldn't you be in the pool?" asked a voice oozing with arrogant confidence.

"I'm not in Dodge Cove," he said.

"Oh yeah? Don't tell me you're still in Colorado. Did they accept you already? That's so awesome."

The words were like a punch in the gut. "Believe it or not, I'm actually in Paris."

"Holy shit." The guy laughed. "Preston Grant actually traveling and not swimming? Should I prepare for the end of the world?"

"Fuck you. I already did my hundred laps, so no need to panic."

"Wouldn't expect anything less." A pause.

"Did I get my days mixed up again? I was pretty sure this call wasn't supposed to happen for another week."

"Is it wrong that I really wanted to hear your voice? I missed you." The guy on the other end made exaggerated kissing sounds.

"You're such an asshole."

"I love you too, man."

Preston threw his head back and laughed. He still considered Jackson Mallory a friend, despite the fact that Tash's ex was persona non grata in DoCo. The internationally acclaimed DJ traveled the world, living it up. It was something Preston envied. The freedom. But he had swimming. There was a huge amount of traveling involved there too. *If* he got into the Bennett Club.

"Why the hell are you in Paris, anyway?"

"Nathan got it into his head to distract me," he said.

"From what?"

He let out a long breath. "Results don't come out until the end of September."

"Ah." Cocky confidence quickly turned into sympathy. "You know he's just looking out for you, right?"

"I really don't need this from you right now." He scratched the back of his head, looking up at the clear sky. Guilt cramped up his already tense muscles.

"Look, I get it. Swimming is your life."

"Like EDM is yours."

"No. Creating electric dance music is a means to an end for me. It's something I love doing, and I'm great at it, but I'm pretty sure that I can find something else if I need to. Can you say the same?"

The fear that scrambled through his veins almost brought Preston to his knees. He didn't even want to think along those lines. Hadn't since he had torn his rotator cuff.

He closed his free hand around the balcony's railing. "Don't even go there, man."

"All I'm saying is maybe Nathan is doing a good thing taking you out of Dodge Cove."

Preston knew what Jackson had left unsaid. They all knew he had the tendency to become hyper-focused. He had been denying it on principle since this trip started, not willing to give Nathan the satisfaction of knowing he had been right.

"Do I suck at listening?" he asked.

"What?"

"You heard me." But he repeated it anyway. "Listening. Do. I. Suck. At. It?"

"You've got to give me more info than that, bud."

"Nate's pissed because I zoned out after lunch." A hoot from the other end forced him to pull the phone away from his ear. "You don't have to be an ass about it."

"Who are you talking to?" came the question from behind him.

Preston whirled around to see Nathan standing in the middle of the living room with his arms crossed, staring daggers at him.

"I gotta go, man," he said, and ended the call. To Nathan he said, "No one."

His eyes narrowed. "Then why hide it?"

"I thought you wanted to be alone."

"Don't distract me away from this. Who were you talking to?"

Already seeing the fight about to happen, like a traffic accident he couldn't do anything to stop, Preston sighed. Nathan was bound to find out anyway. "Jackson."

The silence from his friend lasted so long Preston actually got it in his head that maybe everything was okay. That was, until . . .

"How long?"

"How long what?" he asked back.

"Don't act dumb."

A chill ran up Preston's spine. "Since about a month after he left."

"A month? A month!" Nathan began pacing, throwing his hands in the air as he spoke. "You mean to tell me you've been talking to Jackson for five months?"

"Only once a month. Sometimes two," he said, completely missing the rising annoyance in Nathan's tone. "The guy's pretty busy."

"I don't give a damn how busy the guy is. I was just on the phone with Tash, who was telling me about how love is like acid, and here you are talking like everything is okay."

"He's still my friend," Preston said, going on the defensive. "I know what happened. Believe me, I know. I was there."

"Tell that to Tash."

"I get it. She's hurt. But I also have to respect the guy for pursuing his dream. I'm doing the same thing."

"If that's the case, then he should have told us. We would have understood. Natasha would have understood."

Preston's lips thinned into a grim line. "Maybe there are some things people won't understand no matter how much you explain it to them."

Nathan opened his mouth, but no words came out.

Preston reached out as if to touch him, even though they were standing on opposite ends of the room. "It was a shitty thing he did—"

He didn't have a chance to finish the rest of what he wanted to say. Nathan stormed out of the living room straight for his room and slammed the door.

Not half an hour later, Nathan grabbed a fistful of his favorite buttery-popcorn-and-malt-balls combo from the bucket that he'd ordered from room service. The salt created a perfect harmony with the melted chocolate. And the crunch. Got to have the crunch. The kind where every chew drowned out the dialogue from *Pretty Woman*. Even if it was dubbed in French.

During the opening credits, he'd sent a quick e-mail to Natasha, explaining the fight but omitting the Jackson details, of course. She didn't need to be flying off the rails from the knowledge that Preston had been communicating with the jerk all this time. He scooched farther into the thousand-thread-count sheets, enjoying the soft mattress.

He stuck his hand inside the bucket and brought another fistful to his lips as he mouthed the lines Julia Roberts's character, Vivian, spoke to Edward, Richard Gere's character. Even in French the dialogue still held up. He hadn't been born yet when the movie came out. It was only because his mother had an almost unhealthy obsession with Richard Gere that he had discovered this movie. Almost immediately something had drawn him to the story of a hooker with a heart of gold, swept up into a whirlwind romance by a handsome businessman. He sighed. No matter how many times he'd seen it, the movie never failed to make his heart flutter.

Like the scene where Edward walked into the lounge of the hotel to pick Vivian up for dinner and he didn't even recognize her until she turned around. Classic ugly-duckling-turned-swan moment. It reminded him so much of the time Caleb first saw Didi at the garden party after her makeover. He knew in that instant that his cousin was a goner. The same thing happened with Edward. The look on his face showed everyone watching that there would be no other woman in his life. Nathan sighed again. That was the magic of *Pretty Woman*. It made him believe in true love and happily-ever-afters.

He was so caught up in the movie that he didn't notice the mattress dip until someone was already plopping down beside him. Opening his mouth to protest between bites of popcorn, the familiar scent of bath soap and chlorine blocked the words from coming out.

Preston reached for the bucket.

"Get your own comfort food!" Nathan said, holding it out of reach.

"But I'm hungry." Preston reached for the bucket again.

Feeling obstinate, Nathan leaned to the side and stretched out his arm away from the other's reach. No matter how petty it seemed, he was not sharing the bucket.

"Fine. If you don't want to give me half of what you've got . . ." Without warning, Preston grabbed his hand.

"What are you doing?" Nathan whisper-hissed.

"All that fighting made me hungry. And since you don't want to give me popcorn, I'm taking matters into my own hands."

Nathan almost lost all coherent thought the second his index finger entered the heat of Preston's mouth. He tried to pull away, but Preston tightened his grip.

"Didn't you learn how to share in kindergarten?" he teased.

"Stop," Nathan said, breathless.

"I will if you share your popcorn with me."

"G-g-get . . ." He swallowed. "Your own."

The grin that stretched Preston's lips prevented air from reaching Nathan's lungs. "All right. I still have four more fingers."

Unwilling to endure Preston's devious scheme to get food, Nathan shoved the bucket his way. "There. All yours."

The bastard actually broke out in chuckles. "You are so easy."

"You're such a jerk," Nathan replied, frowning.

"But you looked so serious about not wanting to share your popcorn that I had to mess with you."

Then Preston smiled. Bits of chocolate clung to his teeth. Nathan snorted in surprise. He had to cover his mouth with both hands to keep from losing it.

"What?" Preston leaned in. "Do I have something in my teeth?"

He knew exactly what he was doing, and Nathan was falling for it hook, line, and sinker.

Barely managing to maintain a stern expression, he said, "You honestly think I'm going to overlook everything that happened today?"

All humor vanished. Hugging the bucket to his chest, Preston leaned against the headboard and sighed. Nathan waited, staring straight at him.

"Look," Preston finally said, giving him a sidelong glance, "I'm sorry."

"You're sorry . . ."

Preston rubbed a hand down his face. "I was stupid for not paying attention. I have a lot on my mind."

Nathan's eyebrow arched. "And?"

"And . . ." Preston let out a long breath. "And I'm sorry for not telling you about Jackson. But"—he finally faced Nathan—"I'm not sorry for talking to him. He's my friend. And once upon a time he was your friend too." He raised a hand, forestalling the rebuttal begging to be said. "He hurt Tash, and you're on her side. I get it. I'm not exactly on anyone's side, but I don't support the way he did things either."

How could Nathan stay mad when faced with an explanation like that? Snatching back the bucket, he grumbled, "Fine."

"Fine what?"

"You better not tell Tash about this, or she'll skin you alive."

"Does this mean you forgive me?"

"For the fights? Yes." He squinted at the flat screen. It was the part where Edward was coaxing Vivian to go back to the hotel room after their fight. "For Jackson? Jury's still out."

"I'll take what I can get."

The next time Preston reached into the bucket, Nathan let him.

Eight

HE HAD DONE all he could.

At least that was what Preston wanted to think as he stared blankly out the window from the backseat of the town car their hotel had provided. In minutes the bustling metropolis built on a river gave way to sweeping verdant landscapes speckled with white from countless sheep. Being in Ireland felt like he was in an old world trapped in time, where every conceivable shade of green could be found.

After four days in Paris, they'd moved on to Cork, in the south of Ireland. Nathan had decided he needed to catch up on his sleep, Preston's mother having kept him up late with party-planning stuff, instead of sightseeing immediately. Not that Preston minded, since he was too caught up in replaying the tryouts in his head. The reality was he could have done better. The lack of an e-mail from Coach Bennett proved it.

He sighed into his palm as he rested his chin on the heel of his hand.

Nathan gave him a sidelong glance, his thumbs pausing for a moment above the screen of his tablet. "What's wrong?"

Preston ran his fingers through his hair, gaze falling. "Do you think I'll get in?"

Suddenly confused, Nathan asked back, "In where?"

"The Bennett Club."

Nathan reached out and squeezed Preston's hand. Their eyes met.

"I honestly think you have the chops to make it onto that team," he said. "Coach Bennett would be a fool not to accept you. Based on the huge banners in his facility, he likes to win. And if he wants to win, he'll need you to do it."

"But there are so many—"

"Where is this insecurity coming from?" Nathan interrupted, his brow creasing with concern. "This is not the Preston I know. You are a champion. You are a record breaker."

"It's just . . ."

Nathan tsked, then fiddled with the screen of his tablet for a few seconds. Then he showed Preston the video he'd cued up. It was of Michael Phelps winning his seventh gold medal.

"This is you in a few years," Nathan said with conviction. "I know you're even better than he is."

"You really do believe that, don't you?"

"Of course I do." Nathan nodded matter-of-factly. "I know

what you're capable of. And anyone who says otherwise will have to deal with me."

"Thanks." Preston grinned. "So are you going to tell me what we're doing here?"

"Cork is such a pretty place," Nathan replied, switching to his phone, thumbs moving lightning fast once again.

"And yet you're not looking at said pretty place." Preston's eyebrows came together when Nathan didn't respond. "Plus, when I think of Ireland I think of Dublin."

"I'll have you know Cork is the second-largest city in the region. There's so much to do here. Don't you want to kiss the stone?"

What the hell was Nathan going on about? Preston tilted his head to the side and gave his friend a look. "Stone?"

"The Blarney Stone, silly."

Silly? The last time Nathan had used that endearment, they were children and Preston had been determined he would hold his breath underwater for five minutes. He had almost drowned, having started swimming lessons only a couple of months before.

"Okay, you're officially freaking me out. What's really going on?"

"N-nothing," Nathan stuttered, still not looking up from his phone.

Crossing his arms, Preston studied him. It wasn't like his friend to stutter. Confidence came naturally to him. In fact, Preston had always suspected Nathan was born confident. Then the thought hit him.

"Is it the luncheon?"

"What?" Nathan looked up again. His eyes narrowed.

"The luncheon. I get that it's a big deal—"

"Of course it is." Finally a stillness came over him that Preston was more comfortable with. "Where are you going with this?"

"Well, you're here when you should be in Dodge Cove, planning it."

"I told your mother I could do both." Nathan lifted his chin in defiance. "And I'm actually doing both. The venue has already been booked, and I've been coordinating constantly with the florist, the caterer, and your mother. Everything is coming along nicely."

Preston snorted.

"Why are you doubting my ability to travel with you and plan the luncheon?"

"Don't put words in my mouth."

"If it quacks like a duck . . ."

Preston shrugged. "Let's just go back. It will be better for everyone. And I promise I won't obsess. You can even take my phone away."

There was a pause as Nathan watched him closely.

Despite the comfortable temperature in the car, a light sweat coated Preston's forehead. He locked his knees and shoulders to keep from squirming beneath the strange sense of tension coming from across the backseat.

Then, just as the silence between them started to feel too heavy, Nathan's eyes widened and he wagged a finger at Preston. "Oh no, you don't! I see what's going on here."

"What?" Preston said defensively. "I was just making a suggestion."

"You can't fool me." The lines that bracketed Nathan's lips deepened. "You're using the luncheon as a reason to cut this trip short. Well, think again. I have everything under control. Thank you very much."

"I'm not saying—"

"Oh, but you are. Do you really think I'm dumb enough to fall for the false concern you're showing me right now? I'm finishing this trip with you and planning that party at the same time, even if it kills me."

False concern? Well, damn it all to hell then. "Fine. Fuck if I care."

"Look . . . ," Nathan huffed, spinning his phone in his hands. "I don't want to fight. We're supposed to be enjoying this trip."

"I wasn't the one who wanted this, but I'm here. But you also have to admit that something's been off since Paris. If it's not the luncheon . . . Are you still on me about Jackson? I thought we were over that."

"This is not about him!"

"Then what's with you?" Preston gestured toward his friend, who, for once, seemed to be at a loss for words. "You're never like . . . whatever the hell this is."

Nathan's mouth was opening and closing like a fish out of water. It would have been funny if Preston had been in a better mood, but right now it was just weird. Nathan always had an answer and a plan.

A succession of pings broke the heavy silence. Nathan practically jumped out of his skin, almost dropping his phone, as something that sounded a lot like a sigh of relief came from him. But then again, it could as easily be annoyance, based on the knot that formed on his brow.

"What is it?" Preston asked, giving him a sidelong glance.

"Your mother."

"Normally that would be enough, but you're going to need to give me a little more info."

Another sigh accompanied by a forehead rub. "She says she's toured the venue."

"That's the Rose Room, right?" In his head, much shoulder slapping and congratulations ensued for succeeding at listening.

Nathan nodded, not taking his eyes off his phone as he typed. "She wants to add curtains to 'fix'—her word—the lighting issue."

"Isn't the Rose Room full of stained glass?"

"Exactly!" Nathan slapped his thigh in exasperation. "I'm letting her know that we can't change the existing structure. That was one of the conditions stated in the agreement to use the venue."

Preston did his best to smother a chuckle with a fist, but failed miserably.

"It's not funny! A thousand miles away and your mother still manages to drive me nuts."

The chuckle quickly turned into laughter. Preston's mood lifted significantly. Suddenly, being in Europe didn't seem so bad. Getting to see Nathan implode while Eleanor Grant drove him crazy was certainly a plus. Maybe his parents and Nathan had been right. Obsessing over the results wouldn't do him any good. And being in Dodge Cove certainly wouldn't help. What would he lose if he allowed himself to enjoy the experience?

But it didn't take long for the green hills to get boring. There were only so many sheep he could count. And with Nathan busy putting out another fire, Preston found himself with nothing to do. So he slid his own phone out of his pocket and opened his in-box.

Nine

BLARNEY CASTLE STOOD tall and proud at the center of four hundred acres of beautiful, lush gardens. It seemed that at every corner flowers bloomed out of the earth in an explosion of color. From the massive trees to the babbling brook running through the property, the grounds were manicured to perfection. Dappled sunlight glinted off the greenest leaves Nathan had ever seen.

Unfortunately, the splendor of the place was having a hard time competing with the turbulence in his mind. What the hell was he thinking? After Paris, one would think that he'd learned his lesson. Keep his feelings to himself. Preston wasn't interested in love. But Nathan was sure they'd had a moment. Why would Preston lick Nathan's finger like that if there wasn't *something* there?

It was driving him crazy. Preston had meant it as a joke. A way to get him to forgive the fights. Nathan knew this. Yet he still found himself in Ireland. Ready to kiss the Blarney Stone and gain the ability to speak his mind. Or something like that. Plus the top of a castle for a declaration of love? In his book that passed for romantic.

"It says here that only those brave enough to hang from the castle's ledge will be granted it," Preston said, reading from the brochure he'd snatched at the entrance.

"Granted what?" Nathan asked absentmindedly.

He was too preoccupied with staring up at Preston's face. Despite the stress of travel, his friend looked more relaxed. He still swam on a daily basis, of course, but that was just to maintain his muscle memory. It wasn't anything like his usual training schedule. A hundred laps a day was like breathing. So Nathan didn't worry much anymore that Preston needing to hit the hotel pool every morning would interfere with their trip. It gave Nathan the time he needed to focus on party-planning stuff. He figured he'd get work out of the way so that once Preston finished his workout, they could enjoy the rest of their day.

"The gift of gab," Preston clarified as they strolled along a path toward the castle. "It says here that you will have to hang off a ledge to be able to kiss the stone."

Nathan tsked. "That's nothing."

"You sure?"

He ignored the skepticism as they entered the castle. He was here for love, and love conquered all — even his fear of heights. It wasn't a phobia or anything, so Nathan believed everything would be all right.

Galvanized by the purity of his feelings, he determinedly

faced the climb that would eventually lead them to the top of the keep.

"I have to admit, this is cool."

The pure joy on Preston's face touched Nathan deeply. He reminded himself to stay present in the moment as they navigated a spiral staircase that took them to yet another level. The last thing he wanted was to miss actually experiencing the place with Preston, who had to crouch through arched doorways. Apparently people weren't very tall back then. Gooseflesh rose on his arms as they walked the corridors of old. Some of the walls were rough, while others were as smooth as polished marble.

They visited many rooms and paused to enjoy the view at each window. The higher they got, the more they could see of the countryside. Nathan began to imagine the castle as it was in its heyday, his mind conjuring up a multitude of maids, warriors, kings, and queens strolling along its halls.

"I've never seen anything like it," he said in awe as they came to a particularly magnificent room with a high ceiling.

Preston looked up and turned in a circle. Then he touched Nathan's shoulder, forcing him to look up at eyes the color of moss.

"Not bad," he said.

Nathan caught himself thinking he could die happy. Finally, the guy who didn't want to be here was warming up to the idea that maybe this wasn't half-bad. And he hadn't looked at his phone since entering the castle. Mission accomplished. Well, sort of.

"Come on." Preston looked over his shoulder and grinned, gesturing toward another door by tilting his head. "We're here."

Nathan had been so caught up in experiencing the castle that he'd totally forgotten the purpose of their climb. He let Preston lead the way. His brain could only focus on moving one foot in front of the other. This was it. The dimness of the castle's interior was replaced by bright sunlight. He squinted against the glare, shielding his eyes by placing his hand over them. A wonderful breeze ruffled his hair. This day couldn't be any more perfect if doves flew in a V above them.

Since they weren't the only tourists at the site, there was a line to the Blarney Stone. Preston kept his body directly in front of Nathan's as they inched forward.

Once Nathan's eyes adjusted to the sunlight, his gaze fell to the back of Preston's neck. His tan stood out against the paleness of his hair. In a momentary lapse of sanity, Nathan found himself wondering what it would feel like to weave his fingers through the blond strands.

Tempted by the idea of touching Preston, he hadn't noticed that they'd reached the front of the line until someone said his name. He blinked back into reality only to find everyone staring expectantly at him—Preston, the other tourists, and the man in a Windbreaker sitting by the ledge who assisted those who wanted to kiss the stone.

"All right," Preston said with a shrug. "I guess I'll go first."

"Wait . . ." Nathan reached out, but it was too late. Preston had already stepped onto the ledge. At the assistant's instructions, he turned around and sat on the edge of the parapet. He closed his hands around the metal bars bolted to the rock face behind him. The assistant placed his arms on either side of Preston's waist and told him, in lilting, Irish-accented English, to lean back.

Nathan's heart pounded against his rib cage. He couldn't find his breath. His chest constricted almost painfully. A part of him wanted to reach out and pull Preston to safety before he plummeted to his death eight stories below. The other part of him was rooted in place, unable to move a single muscle.

The breeze was no longer soothing. It had turned into a gust that dried the cold sweat dotting his brow. He attempted to swallow, but the walls of his throat refused to move. A small keening sound reached his ears.

"Pres," he whispered.

A rush of adrenaline coursed through Preston's body as he lay back and touched his lips to the smooth surface of the Blarney Stone. A sense of danger and accomplishment whirled inside him. Like gaining a superpower, he thought he could do anything. Maybe there was something to the legend.

There were metal bars everywhere. Someone would have to be terribly unlucky to actually fall. It was safe, but he couldn't deny the thrill that still went through him while dangling eight stories from the ground.

He let out a whoop and bounced back to his feet. The other tourists cheered. Even the assistant clapped. Then his gaze landed on a pale Nathan. All his excitement vanished faster than a magician in a cloud of smoke.

"Nate?" He rushed to his trembling friend. "What's wrong?"

Nathan shook his head. His eyes were focused on a far-off point, his pupils tiny pinpricks. Preston remembered the time, as kids, when Nathan had boldly challenged everyone to a tree-climbing contest. Nathan had reached the top first, climbing like a spider monkey. Then, when he had realized he was so high up, he had frozen the same way he stood frozen now. It took the fire department to get him down. Preston hoped it wouldn't have to come to that in this case.

"Nate," he said as calmly as his racing heart would allow. "Nate, look at me."

In the slowest five seconds ever, Nathan's eyes moved to focus on his before he whispered, "Pres . . ."

It was such a small sound, but it was something.

"Happens all the time," the assistant said.

Ignoring the concern quickly spreading around them, Preston bent down and angled his head so he was what Nathan saw and not the parapet's edge.

"Breathe, Nate." He took an exaggerated breath. "See? Concentrate on my breathing. That's it."

Soon shaking fingers reached out and clutched the front of his shirt. Preston waited, unmoving.

It took another couple of seconds before Nathan's breathing evened out enough for him to say, "It's so high up."

"No stone kissing for you." Preston rolled his eyes. "Come on."

"I feel like such a failure," Nathan said once they were back inside.

Preston took the lead, the narrow staircase only allowing for a person at a time to descend. "Shut up. It was really high up. And it said in the brochure that the ritual can still trigger attacks of acrophobia."

Nathan huffed a sad laugh. "Only the brave shall be granted it."

"Huh?"

"Isn't that what you said earlier? That only the brave will be granted the gift of gab?" He sniffed.

"Hey." Preston turned around to face Nathan, making sure to stay a step below him so they were at eye level with each other. "You are not a failure. You don't lose anything by not kissing the stone."

"You don't understand," he said, biting his lip as if to keep himself from saying more.

"Spit it out."

"It's just . . ." Nathan dropped his gaze and sighed. "It's just when I saw you leaning back, I suddenly wanted to pull you up because I was sure you would fall. But I was so scared that I couldn't move. What happens if you're ever dangling from a cliff and I'm the only one there to save you and I freeze up and I can't save you and you fall?"

"Uh, okay. Are you hearing yourself?"

Shaking his head harder this time, Nathan said, "But what if—"

"Nate, focus," Preston cut him off. "You're forgetting who has more upper-body strength here. If I'm ever dangling off a cliff, I can easily pull myself up."

Like he had done at the parapet, Nathan blinked. The clarity in his eyes said he was beginning to understand how crazy he was being.

"Now, take a deep breath. That's it. And let it out slowly." When Nathan had done what he'd been asked, a corner of Preston's lips rose. "Next time no more heights, agreed?"

"Promise." Nathan nodded once, looking steadier on his feet. "No more heights."

"Good." Turning back around, Preston continued their descent. "Let's get out of here. Risking my life made me hungry."

"So not funny."

Ten

NATHAN AMBLED FROM stall to stall in the English Market at the city center of Cork without actually seeing the veritable treasure trove of locally produced specialties and imported delicacies.

The raw ingredients being sold were so fresh he could almost taste the ripe fruits, the greenest vegetables, and the most pungent cheeses just by looking at them. But none of that mattered. Even the market's arched ceiling that let in natural light, the beautifully tiled floor, and the soothing central fountain might as well not be there from his lack of enthusiasm. So much for enjoying this leg of the trip. One snag and everything went down the drain. Again.

Insert laugh track here. He had been willing to let Paris go. One mistake like that was understandable. But Ireland, too?

What the hell kind of luck did he have? Had someone cursed him in a previous life or something?

He hated himself for dwelling. Sure, he hadn't been able to kiss the Blarney Stone. It wasn't the end of the world. He should be on cloud nine over Preston caring enough to talk him out of a panic attack. But no. He couldn't get past his foiled plan.

Preston had just moved to a stall selling freshly made pasta when the catchy melody of Maroon 5's "Payphone" emanated from his pocket. Knowing who it was without looking at the caller ID, he took out his phone and waved at Preston. When their eyes met, he mouthed "Natasha," and Preston nodded before engaging in conversation with the girl manning the stall.

"Hi," Preston said, smiling at the pretty girl, who couldn't have been older than he was.

"What can I do for yah?" she asked in the lilting Irish accent that sounded . . . nice. He didn't really have the proper word for it, but it made him feel at ease.

"I like your accent."

She blushed and giggled. "I betcha say that to all the girls."

The way she said "girl" sounded as if it had an *e* instead of an *i*.

Charmed, Preston cleared his throat and said, "I just meant the Irish speak beautifully."

"Then you should hear us sing."

He leaned in closer. "I was wondering if you can help me."

"Sure."

"You see that guy over by the fountain?" He pointed over his shoulder at Nathan, and she nodded. "He's had a rough day, and I'm trying to find a special place for us to eat."

"Ah." Her smile changed to an all-knowing one as she nodded.

With a heavy sigh, Nathan sat on the lip of the fountain and accepted the video call.

"What's wrong?" Natasha asked as soon as her pretty face came into focus.

He rolled his eyes. "If you're not careful, those worry lines on your forehead will turn into wrinkles."

"Don't change the topic." Although she did rub a fingertip over the pucker created by the meeting of her plucked eyebrows. "My twin power has been tingling all day. Since you're clearly still alive, my senses are reacting to something else."

Another sigh escaped Nathan. "If I didn't know better, I'd suspect we have gypsy in our blood. Between Mom's powers of perception and your uncanny ability to know when I'm upset, I just can't hide anything anymore."

"Is that a fountain behind you?" She squinted those bright blue eyes that were a shade lighter than his.

"We're at the English Market."

"So, what's gotten you so deflated?"

"I'm surprised your superpower hasn't told you about it yet."

Natasha pouted. "Spill or so help me I will take the next flight out just so I can give you a good smack."

Knowing his twin never made idle threats, he gave in and said, "Kissing the Blarney Stone was a bust."

"Didn't I tell you that your fear of heights would be a problem?"

He shook his head. "It's actually not that."

"Then what?"

"Preston went first, and when I saw him leaning over the edge, this irrational thought of him falling to his death triggered a panic attack. All I could think was if he fell I wouldn't be able to tell him how I felt and that if he ever needed my help I wouldn't be able to save him. It's silly and stupid and I'm so upset I'd smack myself for you. I think we're just going to be friends forever."

Her features softened to an expression of sympathy. "Oh, Nate, I'm so sorry. That must have been so scary for you."

"You don't know the half of it."

"And here I thought my whole crazy lady speech about 'love is acid' was what scared you off."

"Oh, you did scare me there for a second. Believe me."

She flashed her most charming smile. It lit up her entire face from the inside out. "This trip isn't over yet. Let the Blarney Stone go. I hear they piss on it anyway."

"Eww!" His face scrunched up in disgust. Then his gaze wandered to Preston, who was standing pretty close to the girl Nathan had left him with. Preston said something, and she giggled. Nathan's grip on the phone tightened.

"What's with the murderous expression?"

Distracted by Preston and the girl and thoughts of how good they looked together, he had forgotten that he was on a call with his sister.

"Preston," he said between clenched teeth.

"What about him?"

"I have to go." He ended the call and scowled just as Preston ambled his way.

"How's Tash?" he asked when he reached the fountain.

"She's pretty," Nathan said instead, nodding toward the girl at the pasta stall.

"Margot actually—"

"Margot?" He said the name like it was a curse word.

The swimmer looked over his shoulder and she waved at them, smiling. Preston waved back.

"Will you stop it!" Nathan snapped.

Preston returned his attention to him. "What's with the tone?"

"Don't pretend like you don't know what you're doing."

"Usually a call with Tash puts you in a good mood. Something happen?"

Oh, something did happen. "I thought you didn't flirt. That love and romance were beneath you?"

A tic began along Preston's jaw. "Who said anything about being against love and romance? I'm not Caleb. I'm just busy."

"Just admit that you were flirting back there."

"Fuck." Preston pinched the bridge of his nose and sighed. "I wasn't flirting. I was asking her if she knew of a place where we can have dinner."

"What?" All urges to kill dissipated.

"She said there's this pub a block away that serves the best steak and Guinness pie."

"Pub?" Nathan's eyebrow arched.

"Feeling stupid now or what?"

Not wanting to reach the point where another fight would break out—because God only knew their conversation was headed that way—Nathan got to his feet and said, "Well, lead the way to this pub."

* * *

— 85 —

The brick-and-mortar facade of the pub blended in with the other buildings on either side of it, tucked away on a quiet street south of the English Market. An all-caps neon sign spelled out LUCKY'S in green. Preston trailed Nathan inside as a gust of wind forced them to rush. The temperature had dropped with the sun.

They looked around the simple entryway. There was a stained-glass window on one side that looked out to nowhere. Beside it was a frame with a man in a uniform saluting and the words IF YOU ARE AN IRISHMAN, YOUR PLACE IS WITH YOUR CHUMS UNDER THE FLAGS. Indeed the saluting man stood beneath an assortment of flags in the picture. And below the frame was a sign that read: GUINNESS SINCE 1759. At the other wall was a tile mosaic that featured different bottles of beer.

"Well, hello!" A woman with flaming-red hair sashayed toward them wearing a half apron over faded jeans. Her black T-shirt stretched over massive breasts. To say she was curvy underestimated the full package. "Welcome to Lucky's. I'm Gwen."

"Hello," Preston said. "Margot over at the English Market—"

"Come for my famous steak and Guinness pie, have yah?" Her smile was just as wide as Margot's.

"Yes," Nathan said. "We would like a table for two, please."

Her gaze moved between them. "Americans?"

"Yes, ma'am." Preston nodded. "We're here for the rest of the week."

"Well, then." She smoothed her hands over her apron. "It's not every day we get such a handsome couple in here."

"Oh, we're not—" Nathan began to say.

Preston put his arm around Nathan's shoulders. "See, honey. I told you we weren't lost. He's been in a mood all day."

"Well, we can sure fix that here." Gwen poked Preston on the shoulder. "You two make a darling couple. I knew the instant you walked in. Well, come, come, I have a table waiting for you."

She turned and, with a sway of her hips, walked away.

"What the hell are you doing?" Nathan whisper-hissed. His eyes looked as if they were about to pop out of their sockets.

One thing Preston hated more than being unable to swim was seeing Nathan mope. Since Blarney Castle, Nathan had had a frown on his face. If pretending to be his boyfriend shifted his mood, then Preston would go with it until he got a smile. Maybe even a laugh.

"Smell that?" Preston sniffed the air. Scents of barley mixed with sautéing garlic and onions and all the good things a person could eat and drink. "I love this place already."

He ushered Nathan after Gwen into the dark-wood interior. A massive bar took up half the floor area. The space wasn't big at all, giving the place a cozy atmosphere. The wood gleamed around them, set off by soft lighting coming from an iron chandelier. Gwen stopped at a table nestled in a warm corner, surrounded by magnificent stained-glass windows.

Nathan reluctantly took a seat. Every inch of his body seemed aflame.

"Now, will you let me order for you?" Gwen asked. "I have a special meal I have planned for lovebirds."

Nathan barely stifled a flinch at the word *lovebirds* as Preston nodded, thanking Gwen. It was ironic that the glass windows depicted couples in amorous embraces while Nathan inwardly freaked out about Preston pretending to be his boyfriend. Where had that come from? It was like the universe was mocking him.

When the words "green beer" left Gwen's lips, his attention returned to the conversation. "I'm not drinking tonight, thank you."

"We can make it out of ginger ale if you prefer."

He nodded as she finished jotting down the order, then sauntered away. Preston shrugged out of his jacket and leaned back, taking in the place.

Not knowing what to do with the silence between them that wasn't exactly awkward but wasn't entirely comfortable either, Nathan asked, "What did Gwen order for us?"

A delectable smirk gave Preston's features a roguish edge. "Steak and Guinness pie, of course. Then Irish coffee and Guinness cake for dessert."

At the mention of Guinness, Nathan groaned. "You're trying to get me drunk, aren't you? Just admit it."

"It's just the Irish coffee. The alcohol in the Guinness is burned away in the cooking process. You won't get more than a buzz." Preston reached across the table and brought Nathan's knuckles to his lips.

Nathan pulled his hand away as if burned, despite the ripple of pleasure running all over his body. "Stop it."

"What?" he asked.

"Stop making an ass of yourself."

"That's not—"

"Here yah go," Gwen said, interrupting the rest of what Preston was saying as she set down two heaping plates of her famous steak and Guinness pie and what looked like gallon-sized pints of the green beer and green ginger ale.

"Enjoy," she said jovially, and left them to their dinner.

Nathan waited for Preston to finish what he had been about to say, but the other boy's attention was fully captured by all the food.

Preston brought a forkful of beef into his mouth and closed his eyes. "Mmm. This is *so* good."

Amazed by his reaction, Nathan brought his own spoon to his mouth. He all but forgot that their previous conversation had been left unfinished. The meat was so tender it almost melted on his tongue. The stew was thick with the taste of onions and rosemary and thyme. His eyes practically rolled to the back of his head the moment he tasted the robustness of the Guinness. Preston was right, damn it! The alcohol was gone, but the creamy, spicy flavor of the brew remained. It was like coffee and chocolate mixed together with Worcestershire sauce. Sounded disgusting, but was actually good.

"I wasn't making an ass of myself." Preston took a long draft of his beer.

"I'm sorry?" Nathan tilted his head.

"Earlier, you said I was making an ass of myself."

Ah, what was left unsaid before the food came. "And what do you call all that?"

"An attempt to make you smile."

The green ginger ale went down the wrong pipe, causing Nathan to lapse into a coughing fit that prevented an answer. Good thing too, because he had no idea how he should respond.

"From the looks of your plates, it's safe to say you like the food," Gwen said as she swapped their empty dishes for a single slice of Guinness cake and two glasses of Irish coffee with whipped cream on top. "Are you all right, m'dear?"

Nathan coughed one more time, then squeaked out, "Fine. Just fine."

"Well, dessert is on the house."

"Gwen, you're so sweet," Preston said, picking up a fork and taking a bite of the cake.

She giggled. "You two just look so adorable. I can't help myself."

Nathan shifted in his seat, unable to meet anyone's gaze until Preston's fork, with the morsel of cake, hovered just below his lips. He glanced at Preston, who had been smiling from ear to ear.

"Here you go, honeybuns. The first bite is for you."

"Excuse me," Nathan said, slapping his hands on the table and standing up fast.

"Something wrong?" Gwen asked, concern all over her round face.

"I need to—need to use the restroom," he stammered out, not looking at Preston.

"Over by the back."

She hadn't finished gesturing before Nathan ran toward the illuminated sign with male and female stick figures. It was a coed bathroom, he realized when he pushed in and locked the door. Not really needing to relieve himself, he stumbled to the sink. He pushed up the tap and cupped his hands under the running water. Then he splashed his overheated face.

Breathing hard, droplets streaming down his cheeks, he stared into the mirror. He couldn't get the words *an attempt to make you smile* out of his head. Clearly all of Preston's pretending had come from a good place. Right? So he shouldn't be pissed. But for a moment there, just a tiny moment, he'd wanted all of it to be real.

Eleven

PRESTON HAD LOST count of the number of laps he'd done. For sure he was beyond the hundred he'd promised himself before jumping in. He cursed with each stroke as his arms cut into the water, propelling him forward. Or was it backward? He was no longer aware what direction he was going. All that mattered was that his body carved a swath across the empty blue expanse. It was the middle of the night. He had the place to himself.

The seclusion should have been a good thing. In this case, it left him to his thoughts and the confusion that roiled within him.

Worst of all, he'd lost all control of his breathing. His lungs burned. His muscles ached. Yet the gnawing feeling that he'd done something wrong hadn't lessened one bit. In fact, it seemed the longer he kept going, the more confused he became. So he swam. Stroke after stoke. Lap after lap. Without a clear end in sight. He might just swim until he no longer could.

What had he done to make Nathan so mad?

The walk back to their hotel that night had been awkward. Nathan had marched ahead without looking back once—arms crossed and back hunched. When they got to their suite, he went straight for his room and hadn't come out. Preston knocked a couple of times, but no answer. He'd even pressed his ear to the door and had heard nothing.

A fight he was prepared for. If Nathan was pissed at him, he was willing to fight for the hundredth time this trip. But the silence? It killed him. Nathan never ignored him. Not like this. The last time Nathan had gotten upset, he'd been watching *Pretty Woman*. If Preston heard nothing coming from the other side of the door, Nathan must have gone nuclear. And that scared the bejesus out of him.

He'd honestly thought he had been helping when the idea of pretending to be Nathan's boyfriend presented itself. He'd even thought Nathan would find his actions hilarious. He had always been a sport, willing to go with whatever. Sure, the plan had worked. Nathan was no longer moping. But he might never speak to Preston again either.

Without intending it, he might have just cut their trip short. As crazy as it sounded, Preston was actually beginning to enjoy himself. Sure, he still checked his phone every other minute, but that was beside the point. He wanted to keep traveling.

A twinge in his shoulder finally broke his concentration. His overtaxed heart slammed against the wall of his chest in panic. Instead of tumbling and pushing off when he'd reached one end of the pool, he stopped. Instinctively, he clutched at his shoulder. He leaned his forehead against the tile and focused on regaining his breath. The scent of chlorine stung his nostrils, and still he breathed. He had to.

"Shit," he said, shuddering.

This couldn't be happening. No. No. No. Not now. His shoulder was fine. All the best doctors and physical therapists in the world had told him so. But they had also warned him about overtraining. That night it seemed he had succeeded in ignoring their warning.

He forced himself to calm down, recalling what his PT had told him over and over. Breathe through the pain. It would pass. Until then, no moving. If there was a tear, he would only know after the initial throbbing passed.

In the meantime, he prayed. To anyone who would listen. He prayed. For his shoulder to be all right. For Nathan's forgiveness. For anything and everything to be all right. He needed it to be all right.

"Pres?"

Nathan's voice cut through the almost overwhelming terror that shook him to his very core. He wanted to reach out. Ask for help. But he was too afraid to move. Too afraid to find out if his career was over.

Over the thundering of his heart came the slapping of feet on tile and a palm on his shoulder, right above his hand. "Are you okay?"

"Wait. Wait. Wait. Don't say anything," he repeated over and over through gritted teeth.

The touch receded.

It might have been minutes. It might as well have been hours. Finally his heart reached a cadence that resembled normal.

Blood no longer pounded in his ears. The water finally felt cool against his overheated skin. The long-awaited recession of the stabbing pain had arrived.

Taking one last deep breath, he prepared himself to move.

"You can do this," Nathan said in such a soft whisper, Preston wouldn't have heard it if the pool area hadn't been deathly silent.

The words gave him the courage he needed, recalling everything his PT had taught him. He rotated his shoulder. First forward then backward. There was a tightness there. Then he reached his arm out to his side, parallel to the water's surface, and completed three arm circles. Again forward, then back. Nothing more than a slight pinch.

Preston allowed himself a sigh of relief. "I'm okay. The shoulder is okay."

"See!" Nathan finally yelled, his worry spilling over. "I knew you'd end up injuring yourself."

"It's not what you think," Preston said.

"Really?" Nathan took a step forward, eyes wild. "If you're not obsessing about the results, then why are you here in the middle of the night?"

"I needed to figure shit out."

"Care to enlighten me about whatever this shit is that you're breaking your shoulder to figure out?"

Preston dropped his arm back to his side and looked up at Nathan through his goggles, water droplets obscuring his vision. "I'm sorry."

His apology made Nathan hit pause on his building tirade. "What?"

He pulled off his goggles and cap. "For whatever it was that made you mad."

Nathan drew the white robe he had on tighter around himself. "You're here because of me?"

A quick nod.

Guilt colored the lines of Nathan's face. "I think I might just be the worst person in the world."

"Huh?" Preston tilted his head to the side. "You really have to fill in the gaps. If you tell me what I did wrong, I'll make sure not to do it again. I promise."

"No," came the breathy reply. "I'm the one who should be apologizing. I know you were just trying to make me laugh back at the pub." Nathan bit his lower lip. "I don't even know what came over me. And now you're swimming yourself to death because of it."

Preston's gut clenched. "Hey, hey. I'm okay."

"No. No, you're not."

"It's just a muscle spasm. I'm sure of it."

Nathan lifted his gaze and met Preston's, remorse still all over his face. "I'm sorry for overreacting. I'll try not to do it again."

A corner of Preston's lips quirked up. "Not going to happen."

"I said I'll try. I never said it would work."

Like a breeze blowing away morning mist, the air between them cleared.

"How did you know I was here?" Preston asked.

"I couldn't sleep," Nathan said. "And I realized that the only way I could was if I unleashed fire and brimstone upon you.

But when I left my room, you weren't in yours. So I figured you were here."

"Oh."

"It doesn't even matter anymore. Like I said, it was my fault. So get out of there and let's ice that shoulder." Nathan stepped back to give him space to push up against the pool's ledge. But just as Preston thought his prayers were answered, Nathan added, "And no swimming for a couple of days. You're grounded until we're sure your shoulder is okay."

"But—"

"No buts." Nathan arched an eyebrow in challenge. "Or do you want to head into the emergency room right now?"

Sucking in his lips to keep from complaining and grinning, Preston shook his head.

"Good. Now come on. I need my beauty sleep."

Preston grabbed the towel he had left on one of the lounge chairs and followed. He still had no idea what had caused Nathan's anger, but he was willing to let it go for the chance to start over.

Twelve

AFTER FIVE DAYS of traveling up and down Ireland, the welcome sounds of Rome reverberated in the air as Nathan paced the entire length of the patio attached to the apartment they'd rented for that leg of the trip. No pool. Preston wasn't allowed to swim yet. Distant church bells clanged, causing starlings to take flight from tall steeples and clay-tiled rooftops. Wild hand gestures accompanied the passionately spoken Italian from locals at a café across the street below. And Vespas zooming by announced their presence with jaunty *beep-beep*s. Nothing in his years of considerable travel experience could ever come close to the vibrant Italian lifestyle.

"People here live with a lust for life that comes straight from their loins," his father had told him when they visited as a family. His mother had protested the imagery, seeing as the twins had been only eight at the time. Sadly, the person Nathan had been speaking with on the phone for the past hour was the complete opposite.

He should have known better than to take the call from Eleanor Grant when he had woken up on their third day with a persistent pounding in his head. He sniffed in an attempt to clear his increasingly stuffy nose.

"Mrs. Grant, if I may interject—" he said, but that was all he was allowed to say.

Preston's mother kept right on speaking. They were three weeks away from the luncheon, and the longer the call lasted the faster his carefully laid plans leading up to the event unraveled.

"I do understand that you're allowed to change your mind—" he tried again, and was cut off before he could complete what he had wanted to say, which was that they had already paid a deposit for the venue and for a million other things like flowers, place settings, and linens.

Something inside Nathan's chest constricted. Good God of Vuitton, he was having a heart attack at eighteen. Hopefully it would kill him. Because if not, he was going to have to fling himself off the patio. Yet he was sure Mrs. Grant would find a way to make him finish planning this event even in the afterlife.

Damn, my head hurts. He rubbed his forehead in an attempt to alleviate some of the pounding in his skull from the construction crew that had decided to demolish his brain.

"I completely understand," he said absentmindedly.

He realized his mistake too late. He hadn't been thinking clearly when he opened his mouth. Everything on Mrs. Grant's side went eerily calm. She said it was good that he understood and that she would expect a new venue and proposal in her in-box by morning. Then the line went dead.

For a full minute all Nathan could do was stare at the screen of his phone. If he threw the device away, would it make a difference?

"Are you sure I can't swim? My shoulder is fine," Preston grumbled as he stepped out onto the patio.

Nathan ignored him, continuing to stare at the screen until it displayed his wallpaper of Adam Levine in a ribbed shirt staring all sexy-like at him.

"Nate?"

"Your mother," he said, voice small and lost.

"I'm afraid to ask."

Nathan finally turned his head toward Preston, who stood by the doorway as if getting ready to bolt. Tears welled in Nathan's eyes as he uttered the words, "She canceled everything."

"What do you mean she canceled everything?"

"All the plans." He swallowed, throat scratchy. "The Rose Room. The orders I placed for flowers and the caterer and *everything.*"

"But isn't the luncheon—"

"Exactly!" A persistent chill rattled Nathan's insides with each breath.

"You're looking a little pale," Preston said, finally stepping forward.

"I think I'm dying. I need to send her a new proposal and new venue options by morning."

Within a couple of steps, Preston reached him and attempted to touch his forehead, but Nathan batted his hand away.

"I need to work." Nathan's eyes scanned the area. "Where's

my tablet?" Then he sniffed, swiping his nose against his sleeve without really thinking about it other than catching the bit of moisture that had refused to stay in.

Apparently not getting that Nathan needed to work, Preston reached out again and touched his forehead. "You're burning up!"

"I'm fine. I need to get this proposal done."

"No." Preston wrapped a large hand around his arm. "You're clearly sick."

Nathan used what little strength he had to pull away. "If I don't send in this proposal, I might as well say good-bye to my party-planning dreams."

"Nate, I need to get you into bed."

"No!" He wobbled on his feet slightly. Through the fever fog the idea came to him. "Better yet, ready the plane. You're getting your wish. We're heading back to Dodge Cove."

Preston narrowed those green eyes and thinned his lips. "Can you hear yourself right now?"

Yes. Actually he could, despite the ringing in his ears. Yet he still said, "It was crazy to think I could plan one of the most important events of my career from overseas. We are going home!"

"Nate, you're running a fever." Preston softened his expression, his tone coaxing. "You still have a lot of time. Get some rest now, and I promise once you get better, if you still want to go, we'll be on that plane."

"No. Leave. Now."

"If you promise to be good, I'll get you that chocolate truffle gelato you like from that artisanal place around the corner."

"With a scoop of macadamia too? You know I like to mix them together."

Preston chuckled. "Sure, a scoop of that too, but you'll have to get better first."

The pout came out before Nathan could stop it. "Now you're just treating me like a spoiled child."

"If the shoe fits . . ."

"Hey." But his exclamation didn't have the intended indignation behind it. The pain in his head he had been valiantly attempting to ignore seemed to have traveled to his lungs. Each breath seemed to burn every time he inhaled, yet his skin rippled with chills. Soon he'd be shivering, he knew from experience.

As if sensing the fight draining out of Nathan, Preston reached out. "Come on. You have to lie down before you get worse."

"But the proposal . . ." Nathan staggered slightly.

Preston was right there to catch him, tucking him against his side as he said, "You can do it on the plane after a few hours of sleep."

Nathan nodded as they shuffled their way into the cool confines of the apartment. Under normal circumstances he would be cheering on the inside at having all that muscle pressed up against him. But no. He mustn't let himself be tempted.

"I feel pathetic," he said when they reached his room.

"It's just a fever." Preston's hold on his waist tightened. "You'll be fine by morning, you'll see."

With the last of his strength, Nathan said, "I'll need you to go to the store and grab some fever meds, possibly cold meds, lots of orange juice, maybe a humidifier if you can find one. . . ." He lifted a finger for each item he listed.

"Should I be writing this down?" Mischief accompanied Preston's ready grin.

Nathan scowled. "Oh, and don't forget soup."

Preston said as he tucked him in, "Sick and still bossy."

After giving Nathan a dose of fever meds and making sure he was sleeping comfortably in his room, Preston padded to the kitchen. It was connected to the massive patio, where tenants could enjoy their food while looking out onto panoramic views of the city. The way the sunlight glinted off the terra-cotta-tiled roofs was stunning. He pushed through the swing door and headed straight for the stove to check on the soup he had simmering there.

Steam rose from the pot. Scents of garlic and onions wafted toward him. The broth was a nice golden color. He picked up the wooden spoon he had left on a ceramic plate and dipped it into the bubbling brew. After a quick taste, he added another pinch of salt, the carrots he'd chopped earlier, and the chunks of chicken breast. The noodles would go in last, since he'd bought them fresh and they would cook faster than the rest of the ingredients.

It pleased him that he'd finally gotten to dust off his cooking skills. He had taken summer classes because he'd got it in his head that pizza took too long to be delivered, so he would make his own. After a few lessons, he actually found himself enjoying the process. If he couldn't be in the pool that day, then at least he was being useful.

He replaced the lid over the pot to let everything simmer a little longer, then stepped out onto the patio and stretched out on one of the lounge chairs. Orange sunlight bathed the city.

Minutes later his phone rang. A grin tugged at his lips when he saw the caller ID.

"Hey, man, what's up?" he asked as soon as he swiped right.

"Busy," came Jackson's reply. "We finally made it to Prague. You?"

"Stuck in Rome with nothing to do," Preston answered back, tucking his other arm behind his head.

"I'm preparing for my third show in two days."

Preston could actually hear the stress in Jackson's tone. Was everybody around him freaking out while he was the calm one? Just did not compute. "You're double-booking again."

"And I love every second of it." A muffled discussion followed wherein Jackson seemed to be giving someone instructions. Then he said, "I thought you'd be back in Dodge Cove by now. Finally gave in to the trip, huh?"

"More like I messed up." The memory brought an uncomfortable ache in his chest, which he rubbed at.

"What'd you do this time?"

He sighed. "First, Nate knows that we talk."

A low whistle was the reply. "I knew he would find out eventually. He's pissed, isn't he?"

Preston snorted. "We got into a fight."

"That's rough, man. I'm sorry."

"Second, it's a long story, but I pretended to be his boyfriend."

"Why'd you do that?"

"Let's just say it blew up in my face."

"Of course it did. When the thought to pretend to be his boyfriend entered your mind, didn't you think to consider Nathan's feelings before acting?"

"That's actually what I was doing!" He slapped his thigh. "He'd been moping all day—"

"And you thought pretending to be his boyfriend would make him feel better?" Jackson interrupted.

"At least get him to smile. Instead he wouldn't speak to me afterward. I don't get it. Where did I go wrong?"

A *tsk* came from the other line. "I can't answer that for you, buddy."

"Some help you are."

There was a pause, and then Jackson said, "But I think I have a way for you to make it up to him."

"If it involves apologizing, I already did that."

"No. Listen. I've got these Maroon 5 tickets that I can't use. Give me the address of where you're at and I'll send them over."

"Nate loves Maroon 5."

"Why do you think I'm offering you the tix?"

Preston thought about it for a second. Would Nathan be well enough?

"Funny thing, Nathan actually got sick when we got here."

"You're kidding me."

"And he's been threatening to cut the trip short. Another long story that involves my mother, so I'll shield you from that one."

"Many thanks. Shame to see these tickets go to waste, though."

"Sure, because concert tickets are obviously more of a priority than your friend's health."

There must have been more heat in his words than he had intended, because Jackson's voice was serious when he said, "Hey, you know I'm just kidding, right? Of course I'm worried about Nathan. How's he feeling?"

Preston released some of the pent-up tension that had gathered in his shoulders by rolling them. "Sorry, man. I didn't mean to snap at you like that. Nate's sleeping it off."

"What about the tickets? The concert is tomorrow night."

"We're cutting it a little close, but send them over anyway. This could just be a twenty-four-hour thing."

"You sure?"

"Yeah." Preston shook his head even though he knew Jackson couldn't see him. Nathan might change his mind about going home once he felt better. "I'll text you our address. We're staying at one of the complexes."

"No prob. I'll overnight them. Should reach you by morning." A pause. "I'm really sorry for being insensitive earlier."

"I know. Don't worry about it."

"Do you think if I called him . . ." Jackson trailed off.

Preston knew exactly what Jackson left unsaid. He didn't know why Jackson had run away. The DJ still refused to talk about it, but despite his cocky demeanor, he was a good guy. Unfortunately, right now, the whole of Dodge Cove—with the exception of Preston—didn't think so.

"We're still family," he said, hoping it didn't sound like a consolation. "You never know until you try. Worked with me."

"Let's not push our luck," Jackson breathed out.

For minutes after the call ended, Preston thought about opening his in-box. It would be so easy. Just a couple of seconds and he'd be done.

Lips pressed together, he sandwiched the phone between his palms and leaned forward until one corner of the device pressed against his forehead. *Nah.* If there was a new e-mail, he would have gotten a notification. So he got up to check on the soup instead.

Thirteen

NATHAN BURROWED DEEPER underneath the covers. A vicious shiver rolled through his body. After riding it out, he turned on his side and curled into a ball. The pounding in his head was relentless. How could someone be cold and hot at the same time? The comforter stifled him, but removing it was unthinkable. Another shiver went through him, ending with his teeth chattering. This was probably as close to dying as someone could get.

How pathetic was it that he'd come down with a summer cold the second they arrived in Rome? And right when he needed to work! Mrs. Grant was expecting that new proposal. His career couldn't go down in flames when it hadn't even really started yet. To make matters worse, he could count on one hand the number of times he'd gotten sick. *Ugh!* He coughed into a fist. *Damn. The universe must truly hate me.*

His body hurt like a wrecking ball had hit him. As much as he wanted to climb out of bed and start on a new plan, he couldn't. He groaned as another wave of shivers racked his body. The inside of his throat felt like barbed wire was being wrapped along its walls. Each cough hurt.

Rolling to his other side, he pushed himself to a seated position. He had to suck it up. Just because he was sick didn't mean he couldn't put something together. Maybe he could even send one of the ideas he had banked as a contingency. But the second his bare feet hit the tile, a sudden wave of dizziness had him falling back into bed.

Five minutes. *Yeah*. He'd just take a nap for five minutes. Just until the spinning of the room stopped.

A cool sensation on his forehead woke Nathan in stages. The wooziness had subsided, but his body still felt like a ton of bricks sat on top of him. A menthol scent permeated the air he breathed in. It felt nice going into his lungs. The barbed wire still clung to the insides of his throat, but something eased the scratchiness there too. Maybe he was delirious from fever, but it felt as if he was starting to get better. A miracle! He might just make the deadline after all.

Then the cool something left his forehead. He moaned, his eyebrows coming together in displeasure. Water splashed from somewhere, and then the coolness returned. He sighed. He had his eyes closed the entire time. A little more of this and he would be well enough to plan a hundred parties. Which reminded him, his in-box must be clogged with several unanswered e-mails by now. He really needed an assistant on the ground in case he still wasn't well enough to fly.

But he could worry about that later. First, he had to get well. Fast.

The mattress springs squeaked. Gentle fingers combed through his hair. He reached up to his savior and brought the hand to his cheek.

"Whoever this is, I owe you one," he whispered.

"I think we're even," said the calm, clear voice he would recognize anywhere.

A mix of happiness and anxiety filled his chest. Preston. He had followed all of Nathan's instructions and was helping him get better. The thought awakened flutters of pleasure in his belly.

"Not even two weeks in and already breaking down on me." Preston tsked. "That's a new level of sad."

"I'm sorry."

"If you're well enough to start apologizing for something out of your control, then you're well enough to eat and drink something. We have to get your fever down." A strong arm eased beneath his shoulders. "Can you sit up?"

Nathan had meant everything he'd said. He really was sorry for getting sick, and by extension forcing Preston to stay at the apartment instead of exploring such a beautiful city. This vacation was for him. Nathan silently vowed to make up for it.

Using what little strength he had, he opened his eyes and pushed himself up into a seated position. With sure-handed efficiency, Preston plumped pillows behind him. Nathan waited for the onslaught of nausea, but none came. Not letting his guard down, though, he leaned his head back against the padded headboard. Preston removed the washcloth from his forehead and hung it over the lip of a ceramic water bowl. Then he busied himself with preparing the medication. He picked up a pill and a glass of water and handed both to Nathan.

First was the pill, which he dutifully placed into his mouth. Without waiting, he took the glass and downed its contents. Of course, it was like drinking broken shards, but he gritted his teeth through it and focused on healing thoughts.

"I'll give you another one in four hours. If your fever doesn't go down by then, it's a trip to the emergency room for you." Preston poked his forehead playfully.

"Thank you," Nathan sighed out. "There was a second there when I thought I was going to die."

His nurse treated him to an eye roll. "My mother will just bring you back from the dead so you can finish planning that damn party."

No need to be thinking about that right then, so he sniffed the air and changed the topic. "I see you found a humidifier."

"After putting you to bed, I went to the pharmacy and bought everything you listed. I had to go to a special store for the humidifier." He pointed across the room at the small, box-like machine that was puffing out steam. Then he fussed over the little setup he had on the nightstand. Besides the bowl and cloth, he had menthol ointment Nathan recognized as something his mother used to rub on his chest when he was sick. A part of him wondered if he should ask Preston to do the same. The saner part focused on the other things on the table: a bottle of cough syrup and a couple more ibuprofen tablets.

Seeing Preston care for him with the determination he showed when he trained made Nathan want to faint from the extreme emotions coursing through him. If he'd thought he loved Preston before, that feeling had multiplied by a thousand.

How could he let Preston go without at least trying for something more?

"I never get sick," he grumbled, diverting his thoughts to safer avenues.

"I think the change in weather is what brought you down."

Nathan frowned, considering. "It *was* considerably chilly in Ireland for this time of year, then super humid here."

"You'll be up and about in no time." One corner of Preston's lips lifted. "The soup's ready. I'll go get some. You must be starving."

"You cooked for me?" Nathan's eyebrows shot up.

"I thought I'd dust off the summer cooking lessons," Preston replied with an uneasy laugh. "The store-bought soup just isn't good enough. Is chicken noodle good for you? If you want something else, I can go to the store and grab ingredients."

Definitely swoon-worthy. "Chicken noodle is fine."

"I'll be right back."

Ten minutes later, Nathan brought a heaping spoonful of the soup to his mouth despite the war zone in his throat. Preston had gone out of his way to cook for him. The least he could do was eat every last drop. Even if he winced with each swallow.

"It's not too hot, is it?" Preston asked.

Nathan closed his mouth around another spoonful and chewed on the carrot bits mixed in with the broth, then swallowed and winced. "No. I love it. I wish you'd cook for me more."

His lips wobbled as if he was trying to suppress a smile. "I should let you rest."

Nathan wanted to ask him to stay, he really did. But he was afraid of what he'd say if Preston kept taking care of him. All the feelings welling up were too much.

"Before you go, can you hand me my tablet?" He gestured at the desk across the room. Shifting to work mode always centered him.

"Are you sure?" Preston asked. "The last thing we want is for you to get worse."

"I'm fine." To prove it, he ate more soup, managing to hide the wince this time. "See?"

Sighing, Preston moved toward the desk. "If I don't give you this, you'll just get up and get it yourself anyway."

"You know me well." He set the bowl aside when Preston handed him the tablet. "I really need to get back to work. I promise to finish the soup and lie down if I start feeling wobbly again."

Preston paused, opening his mouth as if to say something. Then, when it seemed like Preston had made up his mind, he turned around and headed for the door. But before stepping outside, he asked, "Do you still want to go home?"

Nathan thought about it. Now that he was feeling better, the panic didn't come. Despite the snags along the way, the trip did seem like it was doing Preston some good. If they went home, the close call he had with his shoulder in Cork might become something to worry about.

The decision was obvious.

"Nah. Let's stay. I can handle everything from here. I blame the panic on the fever."

If he wasn't mistaken, there was a glint in Preston's eyes. Was that relief? Couldn't be. Could it?

"Finish your soup," Preston said as a parting shot. "Call if you need me. I'll be in the living room."

Attention already on putting together a new proposal, Nathan nodded and waved him away.

Fourteen

THE NEXT MORNING, Nathan stretched and sighed. No more headache. He touched his forehead. Cool. No more fever. Then he sat up and scrambled for his tablet, which he'd fallen asleep with sometime after his last dose of meds. He quickly checked his e-mail and breathed a sigh of relief. Mrs. Grant had gotten the proposal he'd cobbled together last night.

With a silent prayer, he clicked on the reply and scanned the message. By the end of it, his smile was so wide his face hurt. The dragon liked the solarium idea. Oh holy God of Prada.

Nathan plopped onto his back and waved his hands and feet in the air, doing a celebratory jig, further rumpling the sheets in his excitement. Then he stopped moving and blinked up at the stucco ceiling. They were cutting it really close with the total 180 on the planning. There was so much to do. Changing the flower order. Changing the menu. Choosing the linens. Scouting the venue. *Ugh!*

Rubbing his face, Nathan slid out of the massive bed and reached for the robe hanging on the back of a chair. An icky feeling caught up with him. Dried fever sweats from the day before clung to his skin. He was in dire need of a shower.

He ambled out of the room and made straight for the luxurious master bathroom with its large brass tub, heated tile floor, and gold-plated fixtures. The patter of the shower running made him pause at the door.

Discarded clothes littered the floor all the way to the shower closet. In lieu of swimming, Preston must have gone on a run, judging from the sweats. No steam rose from the cubicle. Through the glass walls Nathan saw everything.

Preston's body personified muscle definition. Swimming a hundred laps before breakfast did that. Water ran in rivulets down the cuts of muscle on his back. Head bowed, he splayed his hands against the wall as if he needed it for support. The position highlighted the beauty of his arms—the wings he used to fly. Each section—from forearms to biceps and triceps—was the perfect specimen of power. And his legs. Each was a mile long, made lean and sexy by kicking against the pool's surface countless times. His calves were Nathan's favorite—rounded and firm.

He and Preston had shared showers before. And nothing. Just two guys washing away a day's worth of sweat. Athletes did it all the time. But since he'd come to terms with his feelings, seeing Preston naked took on a different meaning. His mouth watered, forcing him to swallow before he embarrassed himself by actually drooling.

Preston turned around, giving him an unobstructed view of the equally gorgeous front. A chest made broad from years of swimming butterfly and abs even a washboard would envy. There was nothing not to like physically. He was the whole package. And Nathan craved every solid inch of him.

"Oh, you're up," Preston said.

Nathan immediately yanked his eyes back up to meet Preston's gaze. Oh, he was up all right. He cleared his throat and swallowed.

"Uh, yeah." He tugged at the robe's belt just to give his hands something to do rather than flail for getting caught leering. "Wanted a shower before breakfast."

"All right." Preston turned back around and twisted the tap closed. Then he said over his shoulder, "Can you hand me a towel?"

At first the request didn't compute. Nathan was too focused on watching Preston open the door to the shower closet. Gods, even water dripping down his chest was sexy. Without thinking, the tip of his tongue darted across his lower lip. Suddenly the bathroom seemed stifling.

"Nate?"

"Huh?" He blinked. "What did you say?"

A smirk stretched across Preston's lips as he pointed to the rack Nathan was standing beside. "The towel?"

"Oh!" He quickly grabbed one from the stack and threw it.

Preston caught the towel, then wrapped it around his waist as he stepped out of the shower. "Anything specific you want for breakfast? I can cook while you shower."

Thoughts of food flew over Nathan's head. Being hit by the full force of Preston just out of the shower was staggering. All that gorgeous sun-kissed hair falling in wet waves over his equally gorgeous face? He could already see the endorsement deals for underwear ads once Preston became famous.

His throat—among other parts of his body—was suddenly tight, so he refocused his attention to someplace safer, like Preston's eyes. Holy Mother of Versace. Had they always been so clear? And sexy? Okay, this was his personal brand of exquisite torture.

"Nate?" Preston reached up and ran his fingers through those dripping strands.

"Aren't you cold?" Nathan managed to ask through a mouth dryer than the Sahara. Without meaning to, he reached out and twirled his forefinger around a strand that fell out of place from Preston's previous combing. Like he'd always known, the guy had such soft hair. Perfect for tangling fingers into. Perfect for grabbing. . . .

Words failed him. Failed him bad as images bombarded his weak brain. Forget lustful thoughts. This was downright inappropriate. How easy would it be to undo the towel and let it fall to the floor?

He had to get a grip.

In an unexpected move, Preston grabbed Nathan's hand and held it. A part of Nathan protested. He wasn't nearly done fondling Preston's hair. Yes, fondling. Because he wasn't thinking with his head anymore. *What would those firm lips taste like?* he wondered.

"Nate," Preston whispered, his face coming precariously close. "You're all flushed. Maybe you need to go back to bed."

The doorbell to the apartment rang, releasing Nathan from the spell that looking up at Preston had cast. He pulled away, took several steps back because soap and the lingering scent of chlorine on Preston's skin—even after a few days not swimming—was particularly alluring.

"I'll get it," he said as he rushed out of the bathroom. He needed the space because he was close to jumping Preston.

Forgetting to check who it was, he pulled the door open to find a deliveryman holding a large rectangular envelope.

"I have a delivery for Preston Grant," the guy said, checking his tablet.

"He's . . . he's in the shower. I can sign for him," Nathan replied, his mind still muddled over what had almost happened in the bathroom.

The guy handed him the envelope and the tablet. "Sign here, please."

Nathan did and thanked him before closing the door. Regaining some of his composure, he returned to the bathroom and found Preston in a shirt and sweats, drying his hair with the towel he'd previously had around his waist.

For a second, Nathan lamented the loss of seeing Preston half-naked, then asked, "You were expecting something?"

Excitement sparked in Preston's eyes. "Are you sure you're feeling better?"

"What does that have to do with this?"

"Just answer the question."

Taking a moment to check himself, Nathan nodded. "Fever's gone. I'm not dizzy anymore. Just a slight scratchy throat, but nothing a few lozenges couldn't cure."

"All right." Preston hung the towel over his shoulders. "Open the envelope."

"Okay." Nathan ripped the top and retrieved a pair of tickets inside. Then his brain caught up with what his eyes were seeing. "Maroon 5?"

"Yeah." Preston grinned. "Jackson had an extra pair he couldn't use. They're playing at Stadio Olimpico tonight."

"Jackson?" he asked in awe.

"Don't be mad."

"These are front row." Nathan's heart slammed so hard he thought he was going to pass out.

"He has his faults, but he's not a total bastard."

"Jury's still out on that." Nathan's eyebrows came together. "But you don't even like Maroon 5."

"But *you* like them," Preston said simply.

Holding the tickets so hard, Nathan practically crumpled them against his chest. It felt like a betrayal to take the tickets considering where they had come from, but this was Maroon 5 they were talking about. Damn Jackson and his propensity for sweetness on occasion. He mentally apologized to Natasha for this slip in his loyalty.

He was so happy the world could have been ending and it wouldn't have mattered—as long as it wasn't before that night. He had a date with Adam Levine. Front-row seats. Close enough that he could probably smell the singer's sweat. *Thank you, Jackson!*

Fifteen

AT STADIO OLIMPICO that night, despite it being the third Maroon 5 concert Nathan had attended to date, the experience was made extra special because he was with Preston. The swimmer wasn't necessarily a music fan, since he dedicated every waking moment to swimming, mentally training for a race, or watching footage of himself in the pool. Even in the gym, he opted to listen to generic electronic dance music, of all things, while working out. He said the beats were easy to move to while running on the treadmill or lifting weights.

Nathan sneaked a sidelong glance at his friend and caught Preston watching him. "What?"

"Shouldn't Maroon 5 be on?" he asked—more like shouted over the loud music—referring to Raging Velvet.

"Oh, right," Nathan teased. "Concert virgin."

Preston dropped his gaze. "Training."

"Well, you're not training right now." Nathan nudged him with a shoulder. "Just enjoy the music."

"But where's Maroon 5?"

"There's always an opening act. They get the crowd ready for the band."

"Oh."

Nathan nodded. Then he began moving to the beat. At first Preston stood rigid, shaking his head. Not allowing him to just stand there, Nathan bumped their shoulders together, then started dancing circles around him. By the second chorus, Preston's lips twitched until a smile formed. He returned his attention to the stage and began swaying to the beat as well. Nathan figured that was as much as he was going to get, but at least it was something.

That night, having the boy he loved go with him to watch what was for all intents and purposes his first crush perform gave the experience a surreal quality. Intense feelings jumbled in his chest. Love for Maroon 5. Complete adoration for Preston. Amazement at this beautiful night. Not once had he thought that he would ever experience something like it. Even if the tickets had come from the guy he'd promised to murder on behalf of his sister.

"Preston, I love you." The words came out before he could stop himself.

"What?" Preston shouted back at him, leaning down. "Were you saying something?"

Nathan pressed his lips together and shook his head. He hadn't been thinking. Maybe because somewhere in the back of his mind he'd known Preston wouldn't hear him anyway.

But saying the words made him realize he could say them. That he wasn't afraid to say them. He just wanted the right time. The right place. Where Preston would hear him loud and clear.

With Preston still staring at him, waiting for a response, he said, "This band's actually good. I think I'll buy their album after."

"Yeah." Preston returned his gaze to the stage, where Raging Velvet rocked the arena.

It wasn't the way Preston said the word that made Nathan's heart beat fast. It was the grin that came with it. This was a totally different Preston. Nathan relished the fact that he could be the only one with the pleasure of seeing him that way. Yet another beautiful memory to file away along with the others he already had.

The roar of sixty thousand voices threatened to pop Preston's eardrums. The experience was surreal. This many people in a stadium made to look like an amphitheater overwhelmed him. Even without looking back from the front row, he was sure nobody sat in their seats. The humongous stage was located just a few yards away from where they stood. Massive speakers on scaffolds towered on each side, and lights shone brightly from the metal rafters high above them.

The energy screaming fans threw at the stage took his breath away. It was totally unreal. They chanted the band's name, fists in the air. His skin tingled, forcing him to stuff his hands into his pockets to keep from rubbing the goose bumps on his arms. He hadn't felt anything like it. Not even while walking toward the starting block before a race. This was a different kind of monster.

It dawned on Preston that he had missed so much because of his training. Sure, he'd been invited to concerts, but he always had to decline because he had practice every day, before and after school, and even on the weekends. At some point he had stopped being invited to things, especially when he had been gearing up for a competition. After all, why would anyone invite him to anything if the answer was always no?

As Nathan swayed to the Raging Velvet performance, Preston found himself studying his friend. In a light sweater and chinos, Nathan still looked put-together. Yet he seemed so different. Caught up in the present. Sweat glistened on his skin.

Recalling their dinner at the pub, sure, it had started out as something he'd hoped would make Nathan laugh, but he couldn't deny that a part of him had enjoyed pretending to be Nathan's boyfriend. Gathering Nathan close to his side with his arm around the other boy's shoulders seemed right. Every touch and smile that entire evening seemed so *right*, even if everything had exploded in his face at the end. He realized, remembering how it had felt to take care of Nathan the day before, that there was another part of him that didn't want to stop pretending.

He glanced down at his palm. His fingers itched to smooth away the tumble of dark hair that had fallen over Nathan's forehead. The feeling both confused and thrilled him. Just like this concert, the feeling was overwhelming, and he had never felt anything like it.

As if sensing him staring, Nathan glanced up and asked, "What?"

"It's just . . ." He cleared his suddenly dry throat. "I've never seen you like this before."

"Like what?"

"Free," he said, finding the word he'd been searching for.

"Finally enjoying yourself?" Nathan asked, eyes gleaming with unabashed pleasure. It did things to Preston. Stirred up feelings he'd been mulling over since Ireland. At almost the same time, they smiled at each other.

"This"—Preston gestured toward the stage, then the crowd—"is fucking awesome!"

As soon as he finished speaking, he went with the first thing that came to mind. He pulled Nathan into a tight hug. While the opening act thanked everyone for coming, Preston continued to hold on. He didn't know what had possessed him to hug Nathan, but as the other boy returned the embrace, a prickle rushed over his skin as excitement coursed through him.

"Thank you," Preston whispered into his ear.

"Hey, I should be the one thanking you."

"That's not what I meant." He shook his head, his chin rubbing against Nathan's shoulder. "Thank you for saving me from myself even when I was being a stubborn asshole."

"What do you say we hit the beach next?" Nathan asked, taking Preston by surprise.

"The beach?" Preston pulled back and met his friend's gaze.

"Yeah." Nathan smiled. "I think you're okay to swim again."

"I think the beach sounds nice," Preston said.

Right at that moment, the crowd began calling out for Maroon 5. It distracted Nathan. He began chanting the band's name as well. Preston stood there, unsure of what to do. He hated that he no longer had Nathan's attention.

A spotlight focused on Adam Levine in a white T-shirt and black jeans. He had tattoos going down both arms, and his head was shaved on the sides and longer at the top, slicked back away from his face. The name of the band flashed on the giant screen behind them.

The scream that came then couldn't compare to anything Preston had ever heard. And he'd thought listening to the crowd cheer for Raging Velvet was as loud as it would get. He actually had to cover his ears. The roar was a physical force—a wall of love rushing the stage. He couldn't imagine how receiving that much adulation felt. The tension in the air shifted immediately from mild euphoria to full-on insanity. The arena practically vibrated.

The Maroon 5 front man hadn't even said a word yet. Preston had expected Adam to greet everyone the way the vocalist of the band before had done. Instead, drumsticks clicked together, counting down. Immediately the group launched into an explosive rendition of their most popular song—fast and emotional. The massive screens exploded into a kaleidoscope of shapes, accompanied by lasers shooting out into the audience from directly behind the band.

At the up-tempo chorus, an explosion of light flooded the stage. Screams of glee rippled across the stadium floor. Preston's gaze dropped to Nathan, who grinned, eyes fixed on the lead singer.

Preston's breath caught as a twinge of jealousy ran through him.

Sixteen

JUST AS NATHAN finished ordering his drink from the sinfully handsome bartender at the octagonal nipa hut bar without walls on one of the famous black beaches of Santorini a couple of days later, his cell phone rang, playing "Love Somebody," his theme song for his cousin's current state of lovey-dovey bliss. It was a video call.

Caleb's handsome face blinked into view a second after Nathan swiped right.

"You cut your hair," Nathan said, noticing the shorter strands immediately.

His cousin combed his fingers through, causing the lush locks to tumble over his forehead. "Do you like it?"

"I suggested it," someone said from the background. Then the phone's camera swung around to reveal the mischievously smiling face of Diana Alexander, aka Didi and the apple of Caleb's eye.

"It's a little too short for my taste," Nathan teased.

"And that's exactly why I made him do it. Never mind that he looks delicious. I knew it would annoy the hell out of you," she teased back with a comical wink.

"I can't exactly think of my cousin as delicious, now can I? We're not in Utah."

"Go back to your painting, D," Caleb said. "And stop talking about me like I'm not here. I thought we already discussed this. I'm not food."

"You're definitely my main course, babe." Didi kissed his cheek so hard Nathan could actually hear the *mwah*. Then to him she said, "Ciao," as the camera swung back around to feature Caleb's smiling face.

"So," he said, lengthening the single-syllable word and turning it into a question. "How's my European adventure going?"

"I'd say the statute of limitations on that ran out the moment you turned back around to sweep your girlfriend off her feet," Nathan said, a chuckle bubbling up from his chest.

"And sweep me off my feet he did," Didi said from somewhere. Nathan assumed she was behind her easel, brush and palette already in hand.

A part of him envied what Caleb and Didi had.

"Did you tell him yet?" came her follow-up question.

His cheeks automatically flushed; then just as quickly all the heat receded. Of course she knew. "Well, no."

Blurting it out at a concert didn't count.

"If you don't tell him, you're forever stuck in this limbo of nothingness. If he rejects you, then you have a chance at moving on," Caleb said, genuine concern in his blue eyes.

"I honestly don't think I can move on."

"I'm positive Preston feels the same way," Didi chimed in.

"What?" Nathan slapped the bar with his free hand. "How can you be so sure?"

"It's my superpower," she declared.

Caleb threw his head back and laughed.

Okay, this conversation had gotten out of hand. Nathan needed to divert their attention before he said more than he had been prepared to say. There was an idea he had been toying with since Rome. With the amount of work still left ahead of him, he needed help. And since Didi had already declared herself a superhero of sorts . . .

"Hey, Caleb, can you put Didi back on for just a sec?"

"Sick of me already?" Caleb asked back, sobering.

The phone was wrenched from Caleb's grasp before Nathan could reply with a sarcastic quip. Didi's face came into focus despite his cousin's protests.

"You summoned?" she asked cheerfully.

Nathan's heart turned to mush for the artist. He loved her almost as much as Caleb did, and she already felt like a sister to him the way Natasha was. Didi was family.

"I don't know if my idiot cousin told you—"

"Hey!" came Caleb's voice.

"We love you," Nathan and Didi said at the same time.

"Jinx!" They smiled at each other.

"You owe me a Coke," she said, pointing at him through the screen.

"I'll owe you more than that if you do something for me."

She grew serious. "Does it involve a body? Because I know the best hiding place."

He chuckled. "I'll keep that in mind in case I murder someone. But no. This has something to do with the luncheon."

"Oh, that big party that Preston's mom is in charge of. Where is that hot hunk?"

"Will you stop it?" Caleb asked from somewhere, and Didi looked off to the side and blew him a kiss.

"At the gym." Nathan grinned, a thrill in his stomach. "Anyway, I need you to act as my assistant. It will come with pay, of course."

Her expression soured. "What's with you Parker men and the need to throw your money around? You know I would do it for free."

"I know that, honey. But this is an official gig. Employees get compensation."

"Well, if you put it that way . . ."

"Can you do it while working at the art store?"

"Of course!"

"Because I don't want you overexerting yourself."

She tilted her head, thinking. Then she asked, "What do you need me to do?"

"Mostly coordination stuff with the caterer, the florist, and other vendors I will be using for the event. Just signing for stuff and making sure that what's delivered is what I ordered for the event. Can you do that?"

"I have the morning shift at the store, but I have afternoons free."

"Perfect."

"I can help her too," Caleb said, after placing a kiss on Didi's cheek.

"Wouldn't have expected anything less." He rolled his eyes at the PDA, which was fast escalating into a make-out session as Didi sat on Caleb's lap. "I'll e-mail everything to Caleb by tonight."

"Uh, sure," Didi said absentmindedly, trailing kisses along Caleb's jaw while still holding on to his phone.

"Got to go," Caleb said, officially distracted.

"Make good choices!" Nathan said as a parting shot, which earned him the finger from Caleb while he kissed his girlfriend soundly.

Once the call had ended, Nathan found himself staring at the pretty pink drink the bartender had set down in front of him. How he wished with all his heart that he would get to experience that kind of love. Didi and Caleb didn't just have a physical connection. They understood each other on a level that allowed them to express their feelings without holding back. He wanted that. Wanted it so much it almost hurt just thinking about it.

Picturesque Santorini.

Preston had never been to the island southeast of Greece's mainland before, but now that he was here, he might never leave. The candy-colored houses seemed to be carved into the cliffs. The sapphire waters of the Aegean Sea called to him. The gleaming white buildings topped with half spheres the color of a stormy sky blew his mind. And the sun didn't seem to shine quite as brightly anywhere else.

Preston had only been to white sand beaches before, so he considered it a rare treat to actually walk on volcanic earth.

Ready to take a dip in the Aegean after an hour of weight training, he ambled his way down to the beach. He followed the path of flat volcanic rock set into the grass until green gave way to sand. He paused at the last stone step and stared. The sand was indeed black. Not as fine as the white sand because of the pebbles, but it was beautiful in its own way.

He slipped off his flip-flops and picked them up before venturing forward. The rough texture beneath his feet made his toes curl. A contented sigh escaped his lips as he tilted his head up toward the clear blue sky. The warm sun kissed his cheeks. It was a perfect day for a swim. In fact, he was raring to go, given that he hadn't been in the water since Ireland. This was the life.

Relaxed to the tips of his toes and his shoulder in top shape, Preston went off in search of Nathan among the ocean of white umbrellas and lounge chairs that dotted the shore. He eventually found his friend underneath the shade of one with his shirt off and what looked like a cocktail already in his hand. His windswept dark hair fell over his worry-free forehead. A gentle breeze danced through the strands. He had his eyes closed, not noticing Preston's approach. He wasn't athletic the way Caleb was. And he wasn't muscular like Preston himself was. Nathan's body was more compact, with lean, sleek lines.

"Do I have something on my face?" Nathan asked sleepily.

"What?" Preston jerked in surprise.

"You were staring at me like I had something on my face."

Shit. What the hell had he been doing? He'd never actually studied Nathan's looks with such laser focus before. Unable to find the right response without lying through his teeth, he did the only thing he could think of. He licked the pad of his thumb, then rubbed it against Nathan's cheek.

"Yeah, right here," he said, clearing his throat.

"Thanks." Nathan rubbed his cheek against his shoulder after Preston finished removing the imaginary stain. Then he stood and offered up his drink. "You should taste this. It's so good I'm thinking of stealing the recipe for future events."

Preston studied the bulbous glass with a curved neck, which had what looked like pink slush inside, a pineapple slice with a pink umbrella stuck to the lip, and a bendable straw. "What is it?"

"Nonalcoholic, if that's what you're thinking." Nathan grinned. "I know you're going to swim, so I'm not getting you drunk."

Tentatively, Preston took the glass and brought it to his lips.

As he was taking a sip, Nathan said, "It's called a Screaming Orgasm."

Swallowing wrong, Preston lapsed into a coughing fit that had Nathan in stitches.

Preston scrambled for one of the water bottles in a bucket of ice beside Nathan, who was completely useless, still laughing at his expense. He twisted the cap off and swallowed grateful gulps.

After he'd downed about half the bottle, he resealed it and swallowed a couple of more times. Inhaling deeply, he resettled his gaze on Nathan, who finally stopped laughing. Well, mostly stopped. Chuckles still escaped his lips as he wiped away a stray tear from the corner of his eye.

"Now, what do you have to say for yourself?" Preston asked in a chiding tone after finding his voice.

Clearing his throat, Nathan said, "You have to admit, it was pretty damn hilarious."

"I guess that's the closest to an apology I'm getting from you for almost *drowning* me."

Fire sparked in Nathan's eyes as he yelled, "I did not!"

Preston threw his head back and laughed. Then he reached up behind him and tugged off his shirt in one smooth pull.

"Are you seriously going to make me apologize?"

"What made you pick the one drink that's made of sugar, anyway?" Preston swallowed again, barely suppressing a gag at the sugary aftertaste still clinging to the back of his throat.

"If you must know, Innocent Passion, which is the real name of the drink, is actually made of a combination of pineapple juice, orange juice, and cranberry juice, which gives it that lovely pink sunset color, along with strawberry daiquiri mix. It also has piña colada mix and a splash of grenadine."

"That's disgusting."

"I can get you something else. Adonis over at the bar knows his stuff."

"An Adonis?" Preston looked over his shoulder at the octagonal structure a few yards away. He studied the man behind the bar, the sudden need to kick his ass surfacing. Where were these dangerous feelings coming from? He'd never seen himself as a violent person, but recently, the instant Nathan found someone remotely attractive, his inner caveman emerged.

"No." He shook his head. "Not *an* Adonis. Although he does look like something that walked out of *GQ* magazine. The bartender's name *is* Adonis. What he must make in tips . . ."

Preston's gaze narrowed as he looked back at Nathan. "Why don't I be in charge of drinks from now on?"

Confused, Nathan tilted his head. "Aren't you going to spend most of your time in the water?"

"I'm not leaving you here alone."

"I'm a big boy," Nathan argued. "I can get my own drinks."

Preston took a step forward until there were only inches of air separating them. Because of his height, Nathan was forced to lift his chin just to look Preston in the eyes.

"Nate," he growled out.

Below the primal urge that begged that Nathan look at no one else but him was something more tender. Something he couldn't quite name but was certainly familiar with. It had come into focus during the concert in Rome. A holding of one's breath. A thrill. The kind of feeling that made him choose to stay on the beach instead of heading straight for the water.

"Trouble in paradise already?" asked an all-too-familiar female voice.

Seventeen

LIKE A TWIG snapping in a silent forest, the moment was broken. Nathan turned to face his sister right about the same time Preston took a step back, bowed his head, and placed his hands on his hips. He was still near enough that when he exhaled, Nathan felt the breath on the nape of his neck. A new wave of goose bumps almost made him close his eyes just to savor how it felt.

"Hello, boys," Natasha said, a smirk on her lips.

She stood like an apparition just outside the shade of the huge beach umbrella, in a wide-brimmed hat, large sunglasses, and a white string bikini complete with a thin gold chain and a butterfly charm around her waist. She hadn't even been in the water and already she rocked the beach, mussed hair cascading over one shoulder. And her skin shimmered. The sunblock she used must have had glitter in it. Perfection. Nathan couldn't have styled her any better.

"Natasha," Preston said, surprising Nathan by speaking first. "It's always good to see you, but I'm curious, what are you doing here?"

"Well . . ." She placed one hand on her hip and played with the tips of her hair with the other. "With Caleb all lovey-dovey with Didi, I found myself with nothing to do in DoCo."

"You were bored," Preston deadpanned.

Her eyebrow rose over the rim of her sunglasses. "I figured with you and Nathan both worrying over swimming and party planning, I needed to come and be the fun police. Now, will you be a dear and go to that handsome-as-sin bartender over there and order me an iced Greek tea with honey? I'm absolutely parched."

Blinking twice, Preston shook his head and turned on his heel. When it came to the storm that was Natasha, it was better to bend with the wind instead of standing firm against it. She wasn't afraid to break anyone. And Preston was a smart guy like that. So, without waiting for another word, he jogged toward the outdoor bar where Adonis was currently serving a gaggle of women. It kind of looked like a party over there. *Good luck to him,* Nathan thought.

"Well, little brother, what do you have to say for yourself?"

He flinched. "Older by two minutes doesn't give you the right to call me that. For all you know, I should have been the one to come out of Mom's vagina first."

Unperturbed, Natasha cocked a hip. "For all you know, I pushed you out of the way."

"Knowing you, that's probably true."

"But I would have said 'Excuse me' first."

"Like a true DoCo princess."

"Well then, come on, give us a hug." She opened her arms wide.

Nathan raced toward her.

Their collision caused Natasha's pretty hat to tumble to the ground, but she was laughing so hard it didn't seem like she cared about anything other than giving him the fiercest hug he'd ever received in his life.

As Nathan set her back on her feet, he placed a kiss on her forehead and murmured, "I'm happy you're here."

When she smiled, it was one of pure love. "Good, because I canceled a couple of dates to be here with you."

"You're dating again?"

"Just testing the waters." After retrieving her hat, Natasha wrapped her arms around his and tugged him toward the lounge chairs. "Will you scoot yours closer to mine? Why are they so far apart anyway?"

Nathan did as he was told.

They sat down just as Preston returned with Natasha's iced tea. Actually, he balanced three full glasses in one hand and held a pitcher in the other. He handed one glass each to the twins and set the pitcher on the small table to the left of Nathan's chair.

"Here," he said. "This should be enough for all of us."

"Us?" Natasha tilted her head at him. "You can't seriously be thinking of staying under this umbrella when the Aegean is waiting over there, are you?"

"But—"

"Ah!" She raised a prim hand. "I don't want any excuses. Go swim. We have much-needed twin talk to attend to."

Nathan bit the inside of his cheek to keep from laughing as Preston worked out what he should do. At first it seemed like he considered taking on the DoCo Princess. But before he could even attempt a verbal sparring match with Tash, Nathan said, "I would go if I were you. She fights dirty."

Sighing in defeat, Preston placed his glass beside the pitcher and turned on his heel once again and headed for the water.

"He's jealous," Natasha said once she was sure he was out of earshot.

Nathan spat the sip of tea he'd been about to swallow back into his glass. Good thing, too, or he would have choked the same way Preston had earlier. "Excuse me?"

His sister twirled a finger in her hair. "Hasn't it ever occurred to you that maybe the reason he hasn't dated anyone in, like, ever is because he's in love with you?"

That did it. Nathan spewed iced tea all over his front. Not very classy at all.

Laughing, Natasha handed him a towel from the stack on her side. He took it and dabbed at his damp chest while setting aside the glass. No more drinking for him. He had a feeling this conversation would take a couple of more turns that would be dangerous for his health if he were currently imbibing liquids of any form.

"Of course, you're the expert when it comes to romance, right? Just because you and Jackson—" Nathan stopped himself before he could finish. Instantly the feeling of being a vengeful bitch for mentioning the one name that was off-limits in Natasha's presence washed over him like a bucket of ice water. "I'm sorry, Tash. I was cornered."

She shook her head so hard he was afraid her hat would come off again. "He made his choice, Nate. You know that. I know that. Everyone in the world knows that." She leaned her head back until her face was tilted upward. "He's living the life he wants, no matter how debauched it might be. I think it's time I put him in the past like he has done with me and start living my own life."

"But the two of you?" He shook his head in sympathy. "You were the golden standard of relationships in DoCo. Everyone thought it was for keeps. Mom was secretly planning the wedding."

"Well, I've seen a ton of photographic evidence splashed across every social media outlet that says otherwise. The guy doesn't even have a type. If it has breasts, he will date it."

"How long has he been gone? Like seven—"

"Six months, eleven days, and a handful of hours if we're using DoCo time," she cut him off, adjusting her sunglasses.

He raised an eyebrow at that. "Well, look who's counting."

"I guess I am. I see it like counting the days of being sober." She exhaled slowly. "Being with Jackson . . ." She paused. "Being with him was intoxicating. I've done my detox, and it's time to move on. So, hello, I'm Natasha, and I'm a recovering Jacksonaholic."

"Hello, Natasha," he said as if they were at an AA meeting. Suddenly his situation with Preston? Not so complicated.

Like she had read his mind, she said, "Don't think distracting me with painful memories will get you off the hook that easily."

"You know I would never—"

"Shh!" She raised a hand in the universal sign for Stop the Bullshit. "If I were you, I would have just come out and said it. On the plane ride over."

"Don't go all realist on me," he chided.

"Look," she said with a sigh that dropped her slim shoulders dramatically. "You love him, right?"

His cheeks burned when he nodded.

"I honestly think you're overthinking this." She pursed her lips. Then she squealed, clapping her hands and startling Nathan. "I know!"

"What?" he asked, clutching at his chest to make sure his heart was still inside.

"I'm taking over."

"Taking over what?" He was almost afraid to find out.

She narrowed her sky-blue gaze at him. "Since you've been doing a piss-poor job at this whole romance thing, I'm hijacking your plans and substituting my own."

"Tash, please—"

"Look, Santorini is pretty and everything, but it's just not my scene. We need a party. A place where you can let all your inhibitions go."

"I don't like the sound of that." He frowned.

Eighteen

A COUPLE OF days later, still reeling from Natasha's sudden appearance, Preston had lost all his ability to speak. Well, not literally. With the twins united, they did all the talking, relegating him to walking a couple of paces behind them as they ate their way along the streets of Amsterdam.

The city of bicycles. There were racks and racks of them on every street. It seemed everyone was either on foot or on one of the timeworn machines. But no matter how many zipped by, they could not distract him from the two dark-haired siblings with their heads together, speaking in whispers. What the hell were they talking about that was so important anyway?

He couldn't understand what Natasha had been thinking. This was his trip, goddamn it! His trip with Nathan. Just the two of them. Not two plus one.

He liked Natasha, he really did, but right that second he couldn't find it in him to do anything but scowl. Every time he tried to talk to Nathan, she was there, hogging his attention. It hadn't occurred to him just how precious those days he'd spent alone with Nathan were until someone else had come between them.

Jealousy with a hint of envy pinched him in all the wrong places. Never had he thought of himself as the type who wanted someone all to himself. But, to be fair, he'd never known what he had wanted until it was taken away. The last thing he needed was to harbor any resentment toward Tash. They were friends. And they would remain friends just as soon as she got on a plane and went home.

Until then, Preston took solace from what the locals called a döner kebab—composed of grilled meat with garlic mayonnaise sauce and chopped vegetable salad, all shoved into a warm pita. Basically heaven in a sandwich and worth each and every bite. The one in his hands had been his third.

"Pres, there's that croquette cart you were looking for," Nathan said, looking over his shoulder at him while pointing at the colorful truck with a long line alongside it.

Preston's heart leapt into his throat and beat there for several seconds. Heat climbed up his neck when he locked gazes with Nathan. He was still the same guy. Well dressed. Hair combed away from his face and tamed with product. That open smile. Yet to Preston, he seemed different all at once. Like he was seeing a new side to Nathan he hadn't seen before.

Natasha stared at him too. The scrutiny in her eyes seemed to pull out all his secrets, exposing them for the entire world to see.

"Uh . . ." He struggled for words around the large lump in his throat. Finding none, he dropped his gaze, nodded like an insecure little boy, then shrugged. *Fuck.* He hated being unsure of himself.

"We'll stay right here," Natasha said. "Why don't you get in line?"

Without looking at either of them, Preston hurried over to the cart and took his place at the back of the line. Nathan's heart sank.

"I don't get it," he whisper-hissed, his gaze boring a hole between Preston's broad shoulders. Then he picked up a fry from the cone he held, dipped it into the mayonnaise it came with, and stuffed the entire piece into his mouth.

"What do you mean?"

Nathan speared her with a cutting glare. "Isn't it obvious? He hasn't spoken to me since Santorini." He gestured with his hands toward the cart.

"Well, have you—"

"Asked him what's wrong?" he finished for her. "Every time I ask, he shuts down."

"Okay." She raised both her hands. "Someone needs to calm down."

"I. Am. Calm." Nathan breathed through his mouth. "You said you're here to help. So help!"

"I told you to trust me. So trust me," she said.

Nathan stuffed his hands into the pockets of his coat in an attempt to chase away the nip in the air. Tash had been right. He needed to chill out. He was probably panicking over nothing.

"Anyway," Natasha said, tugging the collar of her dove-gray

coatdress tighter around her neck. "I maintain what I said in Santorini. You're overthinking things. Preston has always been the quiet type."

"Not when he's with me." Nathan glanced over at Preston again. He was almost at the counter.

"Really?" Tash looked at him skeptically.

"So, why Amsterdam of all places?" he asked after biting into another fry, perfectly crisp and golden. Might as well figure out the whole Preston thing later. They were clearly not getting anywhere with why the swimmer had been acting weird. "Not that I don't appreciate this city. Remind me later to get something for Didi at the Van Gogh Museum."

"Because this is the only place . . ." Natasha turned in a tight circle, looking around and pausing when she'd found her target. She grabbed Nathan's hand and pulled him across the street to a café.

Upon closer inspection, it was actually a coffeehouse. What made him dig his heels in was the cloud of marijuana smoke eddying from the inside.

"I am not going in there," he protested, wrenching his hand from his sister's grip.

"Oh, little bro, don't be a prude. It's Amsterdam."

"You're not seriously thinking of getting high right now." Nathan knew his sister had a wild side, and Caleb had been known to indulge in a little pot now and again, but Nathan himself never touched the stuff. Like alcohol, he was afraid weed would make him lose too much control, and he couldn't have that. One angry e-mail sent to the wrong person or a drunk call made could mean flushing his reputation down the toilet. So, thanks, but no thanks.

"Then stay here," she said, walking in before he could protest. Not a minute later, she walked back out with a brownie on a tissue in her hand. "I just wanted to try one of—"

"Oh, brownie!" Nathan exchanged his cone of french fries for the pastry and took a big bite. The moment the chocolaty goodness hit his tongue, he smiled. Nothing like a decadent dessert to drive away his worries.

"Um . . . Nate . . ." Natasha covered her mouth with a gloved hand, her eyes brimming with shock and mischief. "Well, that's one way to get you to stop overthinking things."

"Huh?" He continued to chew merrily.

She pointed at the brownie. "That's an edible."

"A what?"

"It's laced with pot."

Nathan's jaw dropped. "You drugged me? That's your idea of helping me?"

"No!" She shook her head. "That was for me. Honest. But you took a bite before I could say anything."

"Then you should have knocked the thing out of my hands before it reached my mouth!"

"I'm so sorry. It all happened so fast." Yet she giggled anyway. "You have to admit, it's kinda funny."

Incredulous, Nathan stared at his sister, then at the half-eaten brownie. He'd never been high before. He was with Preston and his sister. Surely they'd stop him from doing something stupid. Right? Plus, Caleb had always been pretty mellow when he'd smoked pot. Maybe Tash was right and this was exactly what he needed to relax?

Nothing he could do about it now, short of puking his guts out. The brownie was too good to waste. So he shrugged, then took another bite. In his memoir, this would be the chapter called "The Day Nathan Parker Ate a Pot Brownie."

"You only live once, I guess," he said.

Natasha's eyebrows rose. "That's what you call killing two birds with one pot brownie."

A couple of hours later, Preston found himself outside Paradiso, a former church turned nightclub on Weteringschans—a street considered to be the center of Amsterdam. A long line had formed around the impressive stone building, with its arched windows and entryway. The parishioners were ready to worship in the new temple of pop and rock at the altar of Jackson. Or as the business knew him, DJ Ax—which was a clever play on the nickname Caleb had given him when they were children. Jax.

"You've got to be kidding me!" Nathan yelled, waving his hands toward the church. "You brought us all the way to Amsterdam just so you can see Jackson?"

Natasha crossed her arms. "I need to do this."

Flames blazed in Nathan's eyes. "And here I thought you were over him."

"I *am* over him." Tash leaned closer, her own eyes blazing.

"Then care to explain to me why we are about to walk into a club just to watch him DJ?"

"Because I want to prove to myself that I really am over him."

Only the certifiable willingly joined a fight between the twins, so Preston stood aside and watched—ready to pull them apart should things turn bloody. What kept him silent was his understanding of where Natasha was coming from. She, of all people, should have been the one Jackson told about leaving. If she wanted to prove to herself that she had indeed moved on, then who was he to stop her?

The doors into the venue had opened half an hour ago and were steadily admitting people with tickets. He silently wondered if they had any, but knowing Tash, she'd bought them as soon as she found out about this performance. She was very much like her brother that way.

"I don't have to explain myself to you," she said, venom dripping from every pore.

"Don't I have the right to understand the insanity of this situation after putting you back together all those months ago?" Nathan hissed. "Or are you forgetting what you did to forget about him?" He pointed at the church.

"Nate," Preston warned.

They were drawing the attention of the crowd. People were actually pointing at them and whispering among themselves. Ugly Americans, party of three. Well, two. Preston was merely a bystander.

"Nate." Natasha sighed and stepped back. She closed her eyes and squeezed the bridge of her nose. When she opened her eyes again, she resembled the cultured socialite Preston was more accustomed to. "I get that you're worried, and I'm really grateful. I'm sorry that I tricked you into coming here. I just thought there would be strength in numbers. But if you'd rather go back to the hotel, that's fine. I can go in alone."

Her calm seemed to deflate some of Nathan's fury. "Just tell me you don't have him on Google Alert again."

Natasha's answering laugh was open and from the heart. She wrapped her arms around her brother's shoulders and pulled him into a tight hug. A small grin tugged at Preston's lips. Good. No bloodshed.

Seeing that the storm had passed, he said, "So, are we going in or not?"

Nathan gave him the goofiest smile ever. "Of course we are."

What struck him as odd was that Nathan seemed a little more high-strung than usual. His movements were jerky, and he had this glazed look in his eyes. And he never smiled that way—ever. Natasha didn't seem to notice as they walked hand in hand into Paradiso and handed three tickets to the man at the door. Preston trailed in after them as they entered the main hall and wasn't paying too close attention until a blast of music slammed into him.

For an instant he took his eyes off the twins. The space was filled to the brim with people. The balconies above them that rimmed the building's interior were also packed. Hands were up in the air. Whoops of joy were drowned out by the live music. The best and strangest part? The lights and lasers seemed to dance in time with the beats. Once in a while a smoke machine would blast white mist into the air.

With his height, he was able to look over the sea of heads toward the lectern all the way down at the front. And there, like the master of this universe, stood Jackson. It was good to finally see him in person after months of phone calls.

Headphones over his ears tamed his usually wild mane of golden hair. His equally golden eyes were downcast as his hands worked the knobs and buttons on the turntables. Once in a while his right hand drifted toward a laptop beside his setup. Even from afar, it was hard to miss the sleeve of tattoos that snaked up his arm. Those hadn't been there when he'd lived in DoCo.

Ultimately, it was the look of concentration on his face that captured Preston's attention. It was like nothing else mattered in that moment. Complete and utter devotion. He'd only seen that expression when Jackson was with Natasha.

Which reminded him, he hadn't come to Paradiso alone. How was he going to find Nathan in all this chaos?

Steeling himself, he plunged into the writhing crowd. After a couple of elbows in the ribs and several heels on his toes, Preston figured out he had to move with the beat to actually get anywhere in that animal house. Every time the crowd parted, he slid through like an ice-skater.

Desperation started to take hold like a boa constrictor when he'd made it from one side of the main hall to the other with no Nathan in sight. He should have been able to find his friend by now. He had all but given up when someone grabbed him from behind and spun him around.

"Preston!" Nathan shouted over the music. "Dance with me!"

Seeing Nathan flushed and excited immediately erased all his anxiety. "You know I don't dance."

"Oh, come on!" Nathan gyrated to the pulsing bass. "Just follow my lead." He turned around and began grinding his backside against Preston. "Put your hands on my hips."

He did as he was told and gripped Nathan's hips and hung on for dear life. Right about the same time, Nathan lifted his arms up and locked his fingers behind Preston's neck.

"Now sway with me," he said, tilting his head up. "Good. That's it. Move to the beat."

Of their own volition, his hands moved from Nathan's hips to his front, and he laced his fingers together against the other boy's belly. He bent down until his chin rested on Nathan's shoulder. Nathan lowered one of his hands to his stomach and entwined their fingers. It was like being in a dream. All the feelings Preston had been puzzling over since Santorini came rushing to the surface.

With his other hand, Nathan cupped the side of Preston's face and said, about an inch away from his lips, "Kiss me."

Nineteen

EYES WIDE, PRESTON hesitated. Had he heard what he thought he had heard? Or was the music just way too loud?

"What?" he asked back.

Nathan turned in his arms. "I said kiss me."

Whoa! He hadn't heard wrong. "What's gotten into you?"

"Honestly don't know," Nathan said. The look in his eyes was even more glazed than before. "My heart is racing, but not in a bad way, and my mouth is dry for some reason."

The moment Preston heard those words, a sinking suspicion hit him. "Come on."

"We're leaving?" Nathan asked, still swaying to the music.

"I just want us to go somewhere private," Preston said as he guided them out of the main hall, preferably to somewhere with bright lights.

The lobby of the church did the trick. It was completely deserted by then. The overhead lighting was more than enough to confirm what Preston had already suspected. Nathan's eyes were red-rimmed.

"Nate." Preston grabbed him by the shoulders. "Did you take anything?"

A confused expression crumpled Nathan's face. "I don't remember."

"Think," he insisted. If he didn't know what Nathan had ingested, then . . . *Wait*. They were in Amsterdam. Weed was everywhere. "Did you smoke something? Eat anything?"

"At the coffee shop," he said breathily, grinning from ear to ear. "It was fresh from the oven and so good. The brownie, I mean. Natasha bought it for herself, but I ended up eating it by accident. Then I thought, why the hell not? And good thing too. I've never felt this relaxed before. It's like waves of bliss are blanketing my body." His words ended in a giggling fit.

Fucking pot brownies. Preston wanted to punch something. What had Natasha been thinking, allowing Nathan to consume edibles? If this was her idea of a practical joke, it wasn't very funny. She knew as well as he did that Nathan stayed away from the stuff. And he'd heard from Caleb that pot was more potent when ingested. Damn it, this was bad.

"Nate, look at me." Even if the other boy complied, his pupils weren't focused. Preston bit back a curse.

"There's something I have to tell you." More giggles, followed by wrapping his arms around Preston's shoulders.

"I think I'll take you back to the hotel." He supported Nathan's weight, snaking his free arm around his waist.

Ignoring the curious looks from the crowd milling about outside Paradiso, they stumbled their way onto the street. Thank God their hotel wasn't too far from the church. He suspected Natasha had intentionally orchestrated it that way. She wasn't winning any points in Preston's book at the moment.

Besides the fits of laughter and the singing and the cracking of silly jokes, Nathan pretty much cooperated as Preston hauled the high-as-a-kite boy into their hotel. The concierge didn't even bat an eyelash at them. But during the elevator ride, the elderly couple they were with gave them disapproving glares.

Once in the hall, Preston dragged Nate by the back collar of his shirt to their door. The almost deadweight didn't help, but it did free up his other hand to insert the keycard, gaining them access into their suite.

Patience wearing thin, Preston pulled Nathan hard against his side, practically carried him into one of the rooms, and put him down. But Nathan managed to get out from under Preston's hold. In a surprising show of strength for someone in his state, Nathan pushed Preston to sit on the edge of the bed.

"I want to tell you something," Nathan said, all his silliness gone.

Before Preston could form a response, the other boy placed his hands on his shoulders, then used a knee to ease his legs wider apart. "Just relax and let me do my thing."

"Uh . . . Nate?"

Nathan winked before cupping Preston's stunned face with both hands and bending down, taking his lips. He applied pressure. In shock Preston opened for him, allowing Nathan to slide his tongue between his teeth to explore while his hands worked on the buttons of Preston's shirt. Then Nathan placed openmouthed kisses along the hard line of his jaw down to the column of his neck. At the rapidly beating pulse at the base, Nathan used his teeth. Preston gasped in surprise.

Taking his shocked state as a cue to continue, Nathan licked at the place he'd nipped, then glided the tip of his tongue along one collarbone as his hands eased the shirt open farther. His thumb circled one nipple while his other hand traced the ridges of Preston's rock-hard abs all the way to the waistband of his pants. Preston sucked in another breath when Nathan unclasped the button and pulled down the zipper, all the while intentionally grazing the growing hardness behind his black boxer briefs.

"What are you doing?" Preston managed to ask.

"I'd like to think it's pretty obvious, considering where my hand is," Nathan teased, but the moment he cupped Preston with the intention of stroking him, Preston pushed to his feet and backed away quickly.

"You're high," he said. "You don't have your head on straight."

"But isn't this what people in love do?"

Nathan's flippant question stunned Preston into blurting out, "What?"

"Pres, I love you." Nathan came closer and glided his hands up Preston's chest to clasp behind his neck. "I've been in love with you for a very long time." A giggle pushed past his seriousness. "Of course, it took Caleb telling me that I was in love with you to actually realize it. I'm hoping that you love me too. Because it would suck if you didn't."

"You don't know what you're saying."

"Oh, honey, but I do." He placed a chaste kiss against the corner of Preston's lips.

No longer able to think clearly while Nathan was wrapped around him, Preston reached up and disentangled himself from the blue-eyed boy's hold. He'd just barely realized that he might have feelings for Nathan, and as much as he wanted to continue, they would definitely regret it come morning if he allowed things to go any further. So, not bothering with fixing his clothes, he ran out of the room toward his own and locked himself in.

Breathing like he'd swum a thousand laps, he leaned against the door. It couldn't be true. Nathan was obviously too high to be telling him the truth. Then his eyes dropped to the object sitting on the nightstand.

A lock?

He moved toward the bed and saw a sweater lying on it. In his hurry to get Nathan back to their suite, he'd accidentally brought him to his own room instead. *Shit.*

Once he picked up the lock, his worries about the room switch were replaced by shock. On the face of the metal were carved his initials, separated by a plus sign from another set of letters he knew so well.

Placing the lock in his pocket, he pulled out his phone. Despite his current annoyance at Natasha for getting her brother high, it was still his responsibility to look out for her. So he sent a quick text to Jackson, informing him that Natasha was in the crowd and asking if he could see that she got back to the hotel safely. Then he took the coldest shower in the world.

Unable to sleep, Preston made his way to the hotel pool and pounded out the excess energy raging through him. But the water failed to bring him calm. Not even the scent of chlorine helped. And no matter how long he swam, he couldn't find the fatigue he needed to rest.

Too many thoughts swirled around in his head. Nathan loved him. He wanted to blame the confession on Nathan being high, but the lock was undeniable proof. That was why Nathan had been pissed about him zoning out in Paris.

At the end of his hundredth lap, he removed his cap and goggles and folded his arms over the pool's edge. Leaning his cheek on his folded arms, he breathed. It wasn't from exertion. He was far from tired. He breathed in the hopes of clearing his mind enough to understand his own feelings. This was all new to him, yet he couldn't shake the thought that he'd felt the same for Nathan and just hadn't figured it out until now.

"You fucking bastard!"

Natasha's voice bounced off the walls of the indoor pool area. Thank goodness it was the middle of the night and Preston was the only one there, because her outburst would have definitely shocked people. It certainly shocked him. He pulled himself out of the pool and braced himself for the irate female.

"Tash, what—"

Her slap across his face cut off the rest of what he was about to say. His head whipped to the side and his cheek burned. He was pretty sure a handprint was slowly forming there. Reaching up to touch the place where her palm had landed, Preston straightened so he faced her once more. She was still in her club clothes.

Her nostrils flared as she spoke. "What the hell were you thinking?"

He blinked, not understanding where the hostility was coming from. "What did I do?"

"Don't play dumb with me." She punched him in the chest.

Preston took the blow. It wasn't as hard as the slap, since that one had her entire weight behind it. "Tash, you really need to explain the slap and why I deserved it."

"How dare you leave me at the club and then tell Jackson I was in the crowd?" she raged, flinging her hands in the air. "And how dare you ask him to escort me back to the hotel? I didn't come here so he could see me. This was for me to move on. Not for him to play hero."

He should have thought first, but her anger was catching, so he said, "And what fucking right do you have drugging Nathan? If I hadn't had to bring him back to the hotel, I wouldn't have needed to text Jackson for help. As your friend, you're still my responsibility."

"I'm no one's responsibility," she said through her teeth. "And it was one pot brownie! *My* pot brownie. That he ate. By. Accident!" She shoved her fingers through her mussed hair. "How the hell are you still in contact with *him* anyway?"

Shoulders slumping when he sighed, Preston explained everything. How Jackson had reached out a month after he had left. How they had begun calling each other once or twice a month since then. With each sentence he uttered, the look of betrayal on Natasha's face was etched deeper and deeper.

"The Maroon 5 tickets were from him," he ended.

"Traitor!"

She launched herself at him. Preston grabbed her wrists when she attempted to kick his groin and shook her. She wrenched away from his hold.

Shoving back the hair that clung to her sweat-stained face, she straightened to her full height. The heartbreak on her face nearly brought Preston to his knees. When he had reconnected with Jackson, all he'd thought about was their friendship and how much he admired the guy for living his dream. Seeing Natasha in pain finally allowed him to understand his mistake. He should have gone back for her at the club after leaving Nathan in his room instead of calling Jackson for help.

"I wasn't thinking," he said, defeated. Was it his lot in life to mess up where the Parker twins were concerned? It had been happening a lot lately.

"No, no, you weren't." She dropped her hands to her sides, then pointed at him again. "If I was a vengeful bitch, I would march up to my brother's room and tell him all about this."

"You don't need to," he said despite himself. "He already knows."

"He knows?" A new wave of rage flooded her features.

"Don't take my mistake out on him. He was just protecting you."

"Like you were protecting me?" She hugged herself. "I'm tired of everyone trying to protect me."

"Then stop doing stupid things."

Natasha looked up at him as if he had been the one who had slapped her and not the other way around. He stepped forward but stopped when she flinched. Even he recognized a wounded animal when he saw one. Had he known Natasha was this broken, he would have . . . what? Stayed away from Jackson?

"For fuck's sake," he breathed, dropping his head. "The punches just keep on coming."

"Well, let me make things simpler for you," she hissed. "I'm heading home on the next flight."

"You don't have to do that," he said quickly, knowing Nathan might blame him for whatever Natasha did afterward. The last thing he wanted was another fight. "I screwed up. I shouldn't have called Jackson."

"Enough." She rubbed her forehead. A gesture so much like Nathan's. "Tonight only proves I'm still not over him. I need time alone. Time to think. I'll write Nate a note explaining everything. Make sure to give it to him in the morning."

Unable to stop himself, and uncaring of the possible fallout, he reached out and pulled Natasha into his arms. She struggled at first but eventually gave in to the embrace.

"You'll be fine," he whispered in her ear.

"How do you know?" she asked, her voice muffled by his chest.

"Because you're strong enough to admit you're still not over him."

She shifted until her chin rested on his chest. "I'm sorry I slapped you."

A small grin stretched across his face. "I should have gone back for you."

"Let's call it even."

He shook his head. "Just say the word and I won't speak to Jackson ever again."

The sigh she let out ended in a frown. "You don't know how tempted I am to actually make you choose sides."

"I'm sorry he hurt you."

"I'm sorry he hurt me too." She buried her face against his chest again.

Preston tightened his hold around her. "I have a feeling everything will work out for the best."

"When did you become so positive?"

He chuckled. "I think your brother is rubbing off on me."

The instant Nathan's smiling face came to mind, Preston knew what he had to do.

Twenty

NATHAN GROANED. HIS entire body felt like lead, from the strands of his hair to the tips of his toenails. Muscles were deadweight. Even his skin felt heavy. Could skin even feel that way?

Maybe he was dead and this was hell.

Deciding to check, he attempted to crack an eyelid. No go. It was sealed shut. Another groan escaped him. The darkness felt extremely claustrophobic, for some reason. The twinge of panic it brought gave him the push he needed to try again.

This time his eyelid opened a slit, allowing in much-needed light. He could do this. He kept reminding himself of that, begging his brain to cooperate with his body.

In an almost Herculean feat of strength, his eye finally opened. He glanced around, getting a sense of where he was. Door. Lamp. Bed. The rug beneath him made his skin itch. No.

Not hell. But not his hotel room, either. Why was he in Preston's room?

And how had he landed on the floor when the bed was mere inches away? Weird. Especially since he was sure he had been standing the night before. When Preston had brought him back to their suite. When he had . . .

This time he groaned for an entirely different reason. If he remembered correctly, he had finally had the courage to tell Preston his feelings. Could have stopped there. But no. He went on and almost molested his friend. *Ugh!* Preston must be freaking out. Nathan wouldn't be surprised if he had taken the jet and flown back to Dodge Cove.

He wanted . . . no, *needed* to be dead. Like right that instant. He had no idea how—if and when he managed to get off the floor—he would face Preston after what he'd done.

One pot brownie changed everything.

Well, that was the last time he was ignoring his gut and using the "you only live once" excuse to try mind-altering substances.

Then the thought occurred to him.

Sororicide—the act of murdering one's sister. A very good idea. The right incentive to get him off the floor.

But wait.

Preston did seem to have enjoyed the kiss. He wasn't exactly pushing Nathan away.

Maybe this could still be salvageable. If he recalled correctly, he did mention something about a brownie. Surely Preston would understand the situation if he explained.

Body. Off floor. First.

* * *

Preston opened the door to the suite to let in room service. After hitting the gym and taking a shower, he'd thought of surprising Nathan with a huge breakfast. Never having been high himself, he'd heard that coming down made people hungry. Last he'd checked when he'd snuck in that morning to get clean clothes, the party planner was still out cold, on the floor of all places. He hadn't bothered putting him in bed. It was punishment for not being more aware of his surroundings.

Natasha had given him the note with instructions not to open it. He promised on his life that her brother would read the letter without any interference from him. He still felt guilty for involving Jackson and vowed he would give him a call when he closed the door to the town car that would take Natasha to the airport. She'd turned down his offer to use the private jet, which he was silently thankful for. He needed the plane for what he had planned.

The fight with Tash made him understand that he didn't want to miss out on loving someone. When Natasha and Jackson had been together, they had been happy. So mad for each other. Preston wanted that. With Nathan.

"Where do you want this, sir?" the man pushing the heavily laden cart asked.

"Let's set things up on the balcony," Preston said, pointing toward the double doors, which he'd left open.

The weather was moderate enough for breakfast outdoors. Nathan would surely appreciate the sun. Preston wanted everything to be perfect.

In his pocket sat the lock. Its weight was a constant reminder of Nathan's feelings. Knowing freed Preston from worrying about his own feelings. Everything had come into focus last night.

As he helped the server set up the table with platters of fruit, plates of pancakes, strips of bacon, slices of ham, a vast array of cereals, carafes of juices and milk, and a pot of coffee, he caught himself thinking that if he had been stubborn enough not to come on the trip, maybe Nathan wouldn't have told him. No more missing out on life. He promised himself that.

It took him an eternity, but Nathan finally managed to get off the floor and onto his feet.

His next order of business was a shower. It felt damn good resting his throbbing forehead against the cool tile and just letting the water run down his back. A part of him was still a bit high, considering the periodic giggles. And he was damn hungry. Like ready-to-eat-a-horse famished. That day calories did not exist in the name of the munchies.

Once out of the shower and feeling almost human again, he realized he had nothing to wear. And borrowing Preston's clothes felt too intimate. Plus, he wouldn't feel himself if he wasn't in his clothes. Even superheroes needed a costume. It seemed trivial, but wearing something he owned would help push down some of the mortification he already felt.

So, in one of the hotel bathrobes, he took a deep breath, yanked the door open, and without looking at anything else, in case someone was in the common room, he ran all the way across the suite until he reached his room.

"Nate?" he heard Preston call from the balcony.

Crap. Of course he would be out there. He had always been an early riser because of his training schedule.

"I'm fine!" Nathan said back. "I'll be right out."

"I have breakfast waiting."

As if on cue, his stomach rumbled.

Preston had managed to stifle the laughter threatening to come out when Nathan finally stepped out of his bedroom. To be honest, he wouldn't have minded Nathan wearing the hotel robe. They were quite nice, and he actually liked them. But knowing Nathan, he wouldn't feel himself not being dressed up. He had always been that way. So Preston had been prepared to wait.

Fifteen minutes later, which seemed like a record considering Nathan's penchant for thinking about what he would wear, the door to his room opened and he stepped out slowly. Preston glanced over at him, and his eyebrows shot up. No wonder Nathan had been fast. He'd just combed back his wet hair. No product. Interesting. He bit the inside of his cheek to keep from grinning.

"How are we doing this morning?" he asked, putting the coffeepot down after pouring out two cups. "Is the weed still affecting you?"

"Is Tash here?" Nathan looked around.

Preston skirted around the table and pulled out the letter. "Here, you need to read this."

"What is it?" Nathan dropped his gaze to the envelope with the hotel's name on it.

"I promised Natasha that you would read this first," he said by way of an explanation.

"Where is she?"

"She left early this morning."

Nathan took the letter. "Why?"

He shrugged. "You'll have to read the letter."

It was obvious from the look of mortification on Nathan's face what was about to happen. Not that Preston needed an apology. But it came anyway.

"I wanted to say how sorry I am for what happened last night," he began. "I shouldn't have eaten that brownie."

"Don't worry about it." Preston placed a hand on the small of Nathan's back. The contact sent a zing up his arm. Nathan looked up at him, his lips parted slightly.

For a brief moment, Preston wondered what those lips would taste like if he leaned in for a kiss. Nathan looked so damn adorable when he was guilty about something. And Nate's cologne. Had it always turned him on?

The need to take things from a casual breakfast to something more was so overwhelming that Preston almost chucked his plans out the window. No. Nathan deserved more.

So, with all the self-control he possessed, he forced himself to say, "Come on, you must be hungry."

At first it didn't seem like Nathan would budge. His cheeks were flushed. Good. He was just as affected as Preston was. It told him he was on the right track.

Then Nathan closed his eyes, sighed, and when he opened them again he nodded as if he'd made a decision. He neared the table and picked up a strawberry. He took a bite.

Smiling, Preston took a seat and busied himself with buttering a piece of toast.

Nathan took a seat as well and opened the envelope.

With bated breath, Preston waited as his friend scanned the note. First Nathan's brow wrinkled, and then his eyebrow twitched.

"What does it say?" Preston asked gently.

"Check it out for yourself." Nathan handed him the letter, then picked up a strip of bacon and began munching on it.

Preston scanned the contents.

In the letter Natasha apologized for allowing Nathan to eat the brownie, that he could kill her later if he wanted, and that she was headed home. That was it. No mention of Jackson.

"Even if she's right about the killing-her part, I'm still worried," Nathan said after finishing his bacon. "It's not like her to just leave without saying good-bye in person."

"She actually did come to say good-bye," Preston said. "You were out cold on the floor. Nothing we did could wake you."

The last part was a small white lie. They hadn't tried to wake him.

Nathan sagged against the back of his chair. "I'm never getting high ever again."

"Look—"

"I'm really sorry for what happened last night," Nathan interrupted, desperation in his tone.

Preston let out a long sigh, pouring milk into a bowl of cereal. It was becoming clear that Nathan wouldn't let go of this until he acknowledged it. Then the thought occurred to him. Maybe he could use this to his advantage.

"Are you mad?" Nathan added before Preston could respond.

"Mad?" It took all his willpower to keep a straight face.

"You have to forgive me. Say you forgive me."

He let the grin come naturally then. "Well, I'm always open to you making it up to me."

The tips of Nathan's ears turned a deep shade of red as he dropped his gaze. "What do you have in mind?"

Preston had to bite the inside of his cheek to keep from saying what was really on his mind in that moment. Instead, after clearing his throat, he said, "Why don't you let me take over the last leg of the trip?"

Nathan squirmed, obviously uncomfortable with handing over control. "What do you mean?"

"Exactly what I said. Let me plan the rest of the trip."

"I'm not sure about this."

"Just give in, Nate. Just give in," Preston said with the most tempting smile he could muster.

Twenty-One

VENICE WAS A haunting place. The snaking watery boulevards made it seem like the city was slowly sinking into the briny depths, but being on a flat-bottomed rowboat gave Preston the sense that everything floated above the water's surface. The fascinating architecture seemed to have withstood the tests of time and nature.

"Did I pick the wrong place?" he mumbled to himself, then gave Nathan a sidelong glance. It seemed his friend was lost in thought.

In hindsight, he'd thought the idea awesome back in Amsterdam two days ago. According to the guidebook he'd read, Venice was considered one of the most romantic cities in Europe. And here he was as nervous as a duck swimming in piranha-infested waters. He had never been the one to carry a conversation before. Hell, he had no idea where to start. How had Nathan done it all these years?

"Did you know the buildings were built on wooden piles and limestone?" he asked the unusually silent Nathan over the too-loud singing of their overly enthusiastic gondolier. To be fair, the man did have an almost operatic quality to his voice. Just too much volume, even if they were outdoors.

"Huh?" Nathan turned to him, blinking several times as if he'd just remembered that he had company.

"Yeah," Preston said, suddenly unsure of himself. *Fuck*. This wasn't going well at all. He couldn't find the right words. So he babbled. He never babbled. "According to the guidebook, the water here has very little oxygen, so the wood hasn't rotted in centuries. Isn't that cool?"

"Sure. Cool."

"And if you notice, the buildings are in the Gothic style that Venice is known for. The arches are elongated and the columns are thinner, giving the city a uniqueness outmatching other cities," he continued as they passed beneath yet another arched bridge that stitched one island to another. God, he was drowning.

Nathan squirmed beside him, tapping his fingers against his knees.

Preston studied him closely. He'd been different since they left Amsterdam. Quiet. Like he couldn't give a fuck where they were. Had it been Preston's fault? Had he done something stupid again? Nathan usually spoke enough for the both of them. Being the talkative one made him uncomfortable. Not knowing what was going on made the situation so much worse.

He sighed. How could he fix this?

The gondolier's voice boomed when he reached the climax of his song, which was in Italian, so Preston couldn't understand a lick of it. This ride was supposed to be romantic.

He had to do something or risk losing this chance. But no matter how hard he tried to think of a way to salvage the ride, no ideas came to his rescue. So he did the only thing he knew to do: changed the pace.

Preston raised his hand right about the same time Nathan faced him and opened his mouth to say something.

"What are you doing?" his gondola-mate asked.

"*Si, signor?*" the gondolier asked at the same time.

"Pull over," Preston said.

"Pres?" Nate looked at him with mounting concern on his pale features.

"Is something the matter, *signor*?" the man inquired, also concerned.

"I read that Venice is a great city for a walk." Preston gestured toward the tourists who were strolling casually along the canal's edge. "I'd really like to try that."

"But the ride is not over," the man insisted. "You paid me handsomely to take you around the best places in the city. We have not made it to the Grand Canal yet."

"Just pull over," he said.

Panic gripped Nathan's heart as the man rowed them to the nearest unloading area. The ride had been going so well. Then he stopped himself. *Oh, wait. No.* Maybe it hadn't been going so well. The moment he'd found out that they were headed for

Venice, his first reaction was, why? They had already gone to Rome. Italy should be off their itinerary. Spain would have been a better choice. Tapas in the afternoon.

But what nagged at him the most was Preston's lack of response to his confession. Sure, he'd been forgiven for going way too far. And Preston still spoke to him. He had even been amiable. But was he sweeping Nathan's feelings under the rug? Pretending the confession never happened? Or, worse, was he silently rejecting Nathan in the hopes he would forget that his feelings were finally out in the open, hanging between them?

On and on his brain went, chewing on the what-ifs like a dog with a bone. If only Preston would say something instead of babbling about the architecture. Venice was beautiful, Nathan got it. He needed more. Like "I need time, Nate." Or "Can we just stay friends?" Or even the expected reply of "I need to focus on my training." But no. Nothing even close to that. And worst of all? Nathan had no idea how to bring up the subject without seeming desperate. In fact, he was already skirting the edge into desperation country, hence giving what should have been a romantic ride around the city only half a mind.

Preston was already off the gondola before Nathan could apologize for being absentminded. Tell him that he would do better. Pay more attention. Then the boy he knew he would love for the rest of his life, regardless of what happened after this trip, reached for him.

Staring at the large hand, Nathan's brain blanked. What was he supposed to do? His gaze moved from the open palm to Preston's eyes. The gloomy weather had turned them a darker shade of green.

"Take my hand, Nate," he coaxed gently.

"Why?"

He wanted to kick himself for blurting out the question. He should have reached out immediately. But instead of being insulted, Preston smiled encouragingly at him.

"I also read that this city was the best place to get lost in," Preston said. "Will you get lost with me?"

For some reason Nathan had the urge to swallow. Who was this person staring down unblinkingly at him? It was as if Preston had transformed overnight into the gallant hero of his dreams. Was this all a trick?

"You're overthinking it, Nate."

Hating himself for being so transparent, he closed his fingers around Preston's hand and allowed the swimmer to help him out of the boat. The gondolier didn't complain any more than what seemed like a proper amount. Like he'd said, he had been paid.

After their gondola glided away in search of its next passengers, Nathan climbed the stone steps of the unloading platform. Once they were at street level, he noticed that they were still holding hands.

"Just go with it," Preston said from over his shoulder, as if he'd known what Nathan was about to say. He tightened his grip as he navigated his way onto one of the smaller side streets between several buildings.

"Where are we going?" Nathan asked, when what he had really meant was, *What does this mean?* But the warmth of Preston's hand seemed so right against his that he never wanted to let go. It was as if their palms were made to fit into each other. Like Lego blocks coming together to create a satisfying *snap*.

"I heard there's this really good coffee place called Caffè del Doge."

"You mean that one?" Nathan pointed at the streetside café with a red awning below the name that had just been mentioned.

"Good catch." Preston tugged him toward the coffee place, with its brightly lit interior and aluminum countertops. "They are like the Starbucks here, but better. I didn't think we'd find one this fast. Luck's on our side."

"But I don't need coffee right now."

Preston lifted their joined hands. "You're cold. You need to warm up first before we continue."

It wasn't the weather, Nathan thought as he allowed himself to be dragged to the counter, where baristas were busy pulling the best espresso shots out of tightly packed grounds from massive machines. What Preston was feeling were Nathan's nerves. He'd been a complete mess that day.

Then the heavenly scent of the richest, creamiest, most luscious cup of coffee made him forget about everything else as he was led to a table for two.

"Did you know a portion of the proceeds go to a nonprofit organization that aids children who work on coffee farms?"

When had Preston become this person who spoke so openly? Nathan had been so preoccupied with his feelings that he'd failed to notice just how much the boy sitting opposite him— who hadn't let go of his clammy hand—had changed since they had begun this European adventure. It seemed so absurd that now Nathan was the one obsessed.

"What's so funny?" Preston asked, watching him closely.

Had he really been laughing? Nathan brought the fingers of

his free hand to his lips as one of the servers placed two white cups in front of them. Instead of taking the cup, Preston's attention was focused on . . . what?

It took him a second to realize that Preston was staring blatantly at his lips. Nathan lowered his fingers and tested this theory by running the tip of his tongue over the bottom one. The green of Preston's eyes was almost instantly swallowed by black. Nathan pushed things a little farther by biting at a corner of his mouth, and the grip of the hand holding his tightened.

The silence between them had gotten so intense that the other sounds inside the café seemed to fade away until there was nothing else but the two of them. Nathan had never seen Preston this focused outside of the pool before. It was like his entire being was attuned to just one part of Nathan's body.

If he leaned in until their lips touched, would Preston pull away? His eyes seemed to tell a whole different story. Could Nathan take the risk?

But no sooner had he made up his mind than Preston let go of his hand in favor of picking up the coffee cup and bringing its rim to his lips. Bereft of the contact, Nathan sought solace from the warmth of his own cup, enjoying one of the best blends he had ever tasted.

Yet at the back of his mind, he knew the dark kiss of the robust roast wasn't what he was craving.

Twenty-Two

GETTING LOST WAS half the fun, the travel guide said. Never had Preston expected the statement to be true while strolling along the labyrinthine streets of Venice. Every time they reached an intersection, they would flip a coin to decide where to go. Heads they would go left, and tails they would go right. Coffee at Caffè del Doge definitely helped. It was like with each sip Nathan rebooted himself, and he was back to his old self by the time they left the coffee shop.

Their wandering led them to St. Mary of Health. The basilica sat on a narrow finger of land that lay between the Grand Canal and the Bacino di San Marco on the lagoon.

"Isn't she gorgeous?" Nathan sighed, staring up at the massive white church with its domed roof. "It's like something out of a dream."

"Give me your phone and stand over there." Preston pointed a few yards away. "I'll take a picture and you can send it to your mom."

Instead of doing what he had asked, Nathan approached a group of middle-aged women who were taking pictures of the basilica as well. He pointed at Preston, then gave his phone to a jolly-faced woman wearing a red scarf. Then he hurried back to Preston's side and slipped beneath his arm. Seeing what he wanted, Preston pulled Nathan against his side. The woman asked them to smile and promptly took the picture the second the corners of his lips turned up.

Nathan retrieved his phone, thanked the lady, and showed Preston the picture.

In the background was the beautiful church, white as a cloud, with statues of angels and saints along its walls, and the two of them in the foreground. What struck Preston were their faces. So happy. Even if he was still a bundle of nerves inside. He was so aware of Nathan beside him that every time the backs of their hands touched, he felt a thrill go up his arm.

Normally thoughts of training occupied most of his mind, but that day his only concern was where they would go next. As enthusiastic as when they'd begun this excursion, Nathan led the way, looking back often and gesturing for Preston to hurry up. And hurry he did, until they strolled side by side.

Minutes later, they stumbled upon the Rialto Bridge, one of three that spanned the Grand Canal. According to the guidebook, it was the oldest in the city.

"I've always wanted to see the shops there," Nathan said.

The energy of his excitement was infectious. Preston allowed himself to be tugged along by the arm.

They walked up the wide steps that would take them across the arch and ambled from shop to shop all the way across the bridge. Some had awnings, while others didn't. Many had window displays that begged passersby to enter to see what else was inside. Then there were stalls that proudly displayed their wares out in the open.

They tried on gaudy necklaces and sunglasses too large for their faces. Nathan laughed at Preston's expense. Preston frowned in mock irritation when a particularly heinous feathered cap was placed on top of his head.

"You honestly think this looks good on me?" he asked.

Nathan took a picture of him. "I think we just found the image for your Christmas card."

"Give me that!" Preston made a grab for the phone, but Nathan danced away nimbly. Preston quickly returned the hat to the stall owner and ran after him.

They stopped at an antique bookshop with an old-timey wooden sign out front and a gondola used as a central display for featured books, besides the floor-to-ceiling shelves along the walls that stretched all the way to the back. They must have spent an hour just wandering the stacks, searching for hidden treasure.

Preston inhaled deeply, addicted to the sweet scent of yellowing pages.

"Do you think Caleb will like this?" Nathan asked, holding up a hardback of *The Great Gatsby*. "It's not a first edition, but I love the cover."

"Get it anyway," he said.

As if those three words had some kind of magical power, Nathan stopped doubting his purchase and headed for the intricately carved counter with an antique cash register. Five minutes later, they were back on the bridge.

At the other side of the Rialto, they found themselves walking down a path so narrow the tips of Preston's shoulders touched the opposite walls. At one point he had to angle himself sideways just to make it to the other end, where Nathan had disappeared. He looked left, then right, a bubble of panic beginning inside his chest. He relaxed only when he spotted familiar dark hair in the distance.

Nathan was seated across the table from an old woman, sipping from a cup of tea.

Taking a deep breath to settle his nerves, having been worried over nothing, Preston approached the odd couple. He was about to draw attention to himself as he reached the table, when the woman took the cup from Nathan and stared inside. She had a Grand Canyon of faces, with lines so deep they resembled fissures. He could barely see her eyes from the folds of skin.

"What is she doing?" he whispered, unwilling to break the intense concentration happening in front of him.

"She's reading my tea leaves."

A furrow formed on Preston's brow as the woman swirled the cup three times and dumped its contents onto the white saucer the cup belonged to. A soft humming sound came from her as she stared at the tiny clumps of tea leaves as if she had nothing else more important to do that day.

"What do you see?" Nathan asked, scooting to the edge of his seat.

"You're not seriously—"

"This acorn," she said in a heavily accented, shaky voice, interrupting Preston's skepticism by pointing a gnarled finger at the upper right of the saucer. "This is a very strong and fortunate symbol indicating happiness and contentment. You will be financially successful."

"Oh!" Nathan clapped once and kissed the tops of his fingers. "What else does it say?"

But before she could say another word, the Wicked Witch's theme from *The Wizard of Oz* filled the air. Preston patted his pocket for his phone, but then he remembered that wasn't his ringtone. At about the same time Nathan scrambled for his phone. There was a summer when he had been obsessed with everything yellow brick road. A spark of mischief went through Preston as he snatched the phone out of Nathan's hand before he could answer it and started running.

"Hey!" came the shout from behind him.

Giddy energy burst out of Preston in chuckles as he looked back from a few yards away to catch Nathan paying the woman, then he started running after him. Knowing Nathan wasn't much of a runner, Preston kept his pace easy, turning around and jogging backward so he could see the annoyance on his pursuer's face.

"Give it back!" Nathan yelled, arms stretched out, fingers grabbing for the still-ringing device.

"Really?" Preston teased. "You picked the Wicked Witch's theme for my mother's ringtone?"

"Well, she's been a complete witch with a *B* lately."

"I should really be insulted." Instead he answered the phone. "Mother—"

"No!" Nathan's eyes looked like they were about to fall out of his head.

He lunged, but Preston sidestepped him easily, laughing as he said, "We're really busy right now. He'll have to call you back."

The gray clouds above them finally made good on their threat. As the first drops fell to the ground, Preston grabbed Nathan's arm. Almost immediately the raindrops turned into actual rainfall. It was as if someone had opened a faucet in the sky.

"Come on." Preston tugged at Nathan's arm. "We have to find a place to wait this out."

"What? Afraid you'll drown?"

"Ha. Ha."

They ran as fast as they could but were already soaked by the time Preston spotted an alleyway that had a balcony right over it. He eased Nathan under the overhang.

Just as Nathan leaned back against the wall, he bowed his head as if he was searching for answers to unspoken questions along the streams that formed on the cobbled street beneath their feet. With droplets crawling down the side of his face, he resembled a sad kitten that had been forced to walk through a storm.

Preston braced his hand against the wall beside Nathan's head and asked, "What's wrong?"

Nathan let out a *tch* sound while his face crumpled in disgust. "You shouldn't have answered my phone like that."

"Oh, come on," he said. "My mother won't think less of you because of it."

Sighing, Nathan dropped his head again. "But it's unprofessional."

"Do you want me to call her back and apologize?"

As if brought back to life by his words, Nathan grabbed Preston's sweater front and shook his head. "That's even more unprofessional."

The air around them grew still. Preston's gaze dropped to Nathan's mouth. The pitter-patter of the rain and other people running to take shelter melted away.

"I've wanted to do this since Amsterdam," he whispered, bending down and pressing his lips against Nathan's.

After a second's stunned hesitation, Nathan snaked his arms around Preston's shoulders and plunged into the kiss. Preston took the parting of lips as an invitation. Their tongues met in a dance that was both new and as old as time. They matched each other—equally hungry to explore and taste.

The mingled scents of rain, cologne, and the musk of the canals created a heady mix that fanned the flames burning in Preston's chest. He wanted . . . no, *needed* more. Hands glided up his shoulders until Nathan's fingers curled into his hair. Encouraged, Preston moved his hand from the wall to Nathan's hip, crushing their bodies together in an attempt to alleviate some of the building pressure inside him. Nathan shuddered at the contact.

His murmurs of pleasure pushed Preston further. Never in his wildest dreams had he imagined that kissing would feel this good. It took over his mind completely, flooding it with sensation after sensation until he thought his head would explode.

He slipped his other hand into the hem of Nathan's shirt. The skin-on-skin contact elicited a moan. From whom, he couldn't tell. It sounded almost desperate to his ears.

With what little control he had left, Preston broke the kiss. Their breaths mingled when they searched each other's faces for the right thing to say. There was no mistaking the desire in Nathan's almost black eyes. Only a blue ring remained.

"Wow," Nathan breathed out.

A grin tugged at Preston's lips. "Now *that* should have been our first kiss."

Nathan bit the corner of his swollen lower lip. "Where did you learn to kiss like that?"

"Swim camp wasn't just about swimming."

"With girls?" He paused a breath. "Boys?"

"Both."

Nathan's eyebrows shot up. "And?"

"I'm here with you, aren't I?"

Grabbing Preston's soaked sweater front, Nathan pulled. Preston bent down and took possession of Nathan's lips once again. Nathan's grip tightened, as he matched Preston's need to explore with a hunger of his own. He took Preston's lower lip between his teeth and traced the tip of his tongue over it. Preston gasped, feeling the touch all the way to the base of his spine.

This time, when Preston broke the contact he made sure to press their foreheads together. He wouldn't have been surprised if steam rose from their bodies.

Breathing hard, he said, "Have dinner with me."

"Are you going to pretend to be my boyfriend again?"

Despite the teasing in Nathan's tone, Preston pulled back and pinned him with a serious stare. "This time it won't be pretend."

Twenty-Three

PRESTON HELD NATHAN'S hand the entire walk back to their hotel. He couldn't find it in himself to let go. Not even when they entered the elevator. Not even when Nathan had to get off at his floor.

"Pres," Nathan said with a knowing grin, his lips still kiss swollen. "You need to let go of my hand."

"What if I don't want to?"

"Well . . ." Nathan pushed up to his toes and planted a kiss on Preston's lips.

Almost immediately, Preston moved to respond, letting go of Nathan's hand so he could cup the back of his neck. Apparently, this was what the other boy had been waiting for. Nathan danced out of reach, leaving Preston cold and wanting.

"I need to get dressed," Nathan said in a playful tone. "And you know how long that takes."

Rolling his eyes, Preston shook his head. There was truth in those words. Yet all he wanted to do was grab Nathan and finish what he had started. He cursed the hotel for being full, forcing them to book separate rooms on different floors.

"This isn't over," he said instead.

Nathan winked. "I'm counting on it."

"Pick you up at seven."

"That's not enough time!"

"You better hurry then."

With panic on his face, Nathan sprinted the rest of the way to his room.

Preston waited until Nathan disappeared through his door. Once it was closed, he turned on his heel and walked back to the bank of elevators. Each step didn't seem to land. It was as if he floated.

He couldn't have planned things better than this.

Speaking of plans, he pressed the button for Up and fished out his phone. Might as well make reservations. The elevator doors opened and Preston stepped in as he looked at the screen. The e-mail icon appeared at the top left corner.

Distracted by thoughts of that night's dinner, Preston opened his e-mail app absentmindedly. His stomach flipped when he read the subject line of the message at the top of the list.

He immediately tapped the screen with his thumb and the letter popped open. His eyes did a quick scan of the words, but the big, bold *Congratulations* might as well have been a neon sign.

As the elevator doors opened at his floor, Preston let out a huge whoop, startling the couple about to enter.

"I got in!" he told them. "I. Got. In!"

The man and woman smiled at him. One of them might have even congratulated him. But Preston's mind was already focused on what he had to do. A mental list quickly materialized as he hurried to his room.

He had to pack, then book a ticket to Colorado.

No!

Book ticket first, then pack.

Then tell Nathan.

Nathan got out of the shower feeling invigorated, like he could face anything that would come his way. He shrugged on the hotel-provided robe and savored the rich cotton against his warm skin. Then he touched his mouth and smiled. He could still feel the softness of Preston's lips. The hot kisses. The cool rain soaking their clothes. The scent of him.

The memory of that kiss was enshrined in the Hall of Fame in his mind. He would never forget it. Even when old age took away the rest, the kiss would remain. He was sure of it as he stepped into the Gothic-style room with its dark furnishings, low chandelier, massive four-poster bed, and gilt mirrors on velvet-covered walls. It could easily have been the gaudiest space he had ever been in, yet it seemed to suit his surroundings. The entire city mirrored the same design, even if the color schemes might vary. He felt like an extra in a historical horror movie.

Moving to the closet, he pulled aside the louvered doors in search of something to wear. They were going on their first date. It seemed funny to Nathan now how afraid he had been of losing Preston's friendship. He should have trusted more in their years together.

He pulled out a blue sweater and a pair of light-gray dress slacks. The combination would go perfectly with the new belt he'd bought at the Rialto and the blue suede loafers with the tassels he'd brought along for the trip. At the back of his mind, he wished for his closet back in DoCo. There were so many more options there. So much more first-date-appropriate attire he could choose from. But, alas, he had no time to go out and buy something new. Preston was due to pick him up in half an hour, and he still had a lot of prep to do.

At first he'd hated that the hotel they were staying at didn't have suites with two adjoining rooms like they were used to. With tourist season at its peak, they had to make do with separate rooms on different floors. In hindsight, the separation added an extra thrill to their situation. Hence Preston picking him up.

A quiver began in Nathan's stomach as he got dressed. Not that he expected anything to happen that night. This was a whole different playing field for both of them. Friends moving on to something more. Maybe Preston would want to take things slow, and he was fine with that. But definitely more kissing.

A knock at the door pulled him away from his thoughts. He glanced at the clock. Preston was early.

Running his fingers through his damp hair in an effort to get the strands to behave, he rushed to the door and opened it.

"I'm not ready yet," he said. The smile beginning on his face froze when he took in Preston's appearance. "You're not wearing that to our date, are you?"

The swimmer was in jeans and a T-shirt with a jacket over it. Too casual for what Nathan had in mind, but he quickly realized it didn't matter. Let Preston wear whatever he wanted. They were having dinner. That meant blue skies and bunny rabbits in his world.

"Well, come in." He stepped aside. "Give me a minute to put some product in my hair, and then we can—"

Preston charged inside the room and picked Nathan up and swung him around in one of those twirling hugs straight out of a romantic comedy.

"Pres!" Nathan gasped. "What's going on? You're freaking me out."

Preston put him down. A smile still on his face, he said, "I got in."

The words didn't make sense in Nathan's head. "Got in where?"

Preston pulled out his phone and showed Nathan the e-mail. The sender's name alone was more than enough: Coach Bobby Bennett. Nathan's eyes skimmed the letter after he'd seen the word *Congratulations* at the top. Preston had done it. Despite all his doubts, he had gotten into the Bennett Club. This was it, the most important step toward his dreams of becoming an Olympian.

Happiness filled Nathan. He knew Preston would get in. He'd always known it.

"Congratulations!" he screamed, jumping in place.

"This is it!" Preston slapped his hands on top of Nathan's shoulders. "This is fucking it! And you always knew, too. You always believed."

"Didn't I tell you? Bennett would have been insane not to

accept you into the club." That was when Nathan noticed the duffel. His heart sank just as fast as the elation had come. "You're leaving?"

He hadn't meant it as a question, since it was so obvious, but it came out that way anyway. It was all happening so fast. He didn't have time to process.

Preston slipped his phone back into his pocket. "Yeah. I have to cut our trip short. You understand, right?"

"Of—of course," Nathan stammered.

"When I got the e-mail, I dropped everything and started packing. My flight leaves in a couple of hours. I need to leave now if I want to make it to the airport in time."

"You're flying commercial? What about the jet?"

"I thought you'd want to take it back to Dodge Cove. I mean, you still have my mother's party to plan, right?"

"Oh . . ." Nathan's smile wobbled. An ache began in his chest. "You should go then. Don't want the plane to leave without you."

As if he hadn't heard Nathan speak—because how could he when he was so hyped up—Preston said, "Fuck. I'm literally shaking. Coach wants me in Colorado ASAP. Training starts in a couple of days. I won't even have time to shake off the jet lag."

"Take an Ambien and sleep on the plane." The advice sounded hollow to Nathan's ears, but the words came out before he could stop himself. No matter what, he was still Preston's friend. And friends took care of each other. But why did speaking hurt so bad?

"A car is actually waiting for me outside." Preston gave him a quick hug. "I just stopped by to let you know."

The contact stifled Nathan. He almost flinched from how

warm Preston's body felt against his. It conjured up memories of rain and kisses. The forever memory. The one that would now haunt him for the rest of his life.

"I'll call you," Preston said as he walked out of the room.

The closing of the door seemed so loud as Nathan whispered, "Don't go."

Twenty-Four

AS IF IT wasn't bad enough to fly home brokenhearted, Nathan had to do it alone. All this time he'd been afraid that telling Preston how he felt would drive them apart. Never had it occurred to him that swimming would be what came between them. It would always be the priority in Preston's life, leaving Nathan feeling like a mistress when really he shouldn't be thinking in those terms.

So, every day for a week back in DoCo, he cried himself to sleep. The kind of cry that left him exhausted until he could think of nothing else. The kind that allowed him to slip into the dreamless black until morning light forced him awake again.

By the eighth day, Maroon 5's *Songs About Jane*—in his opinion the best breakup album ever created—blasted at full volume from all four corners of his room. He burrowed deeper into his sheets as Adam Levine's high-pitched shrieks soothed his battered soul. From "Harder to Breathe" to "Sweetest Goodbye," all the songs spoke to him on a level no one else could understand. It was like Adam had written those songs for him.

He felt so hollow that every time he shifted, his insides echoed. Most mornings he got away with staying in bed, working on Eleanor Grant's luncheon for the Society of Dodge Cove Matrons in the afternoons and well into the night.

There were moments when he caught himself out of order, unable to function, gone fishing. Screw the sunrise and the birdsong. He wished for thunderstorms and torrential rains. Was it too much to hope for an asteroid to hit the earth? It certainly felt like the end of the world.

Another day, another moment without *him*.

Pulling the covers over his head completely, Nathan sighed. His heart shriveled to the size of an ugly prune. Had this been what Natasha felt when Jackson had left? Somehow he had a deeper appreciation for what she'd gone through. Love was indeed acid in the veins. Someone should write a song about that.

He was just about to turn over when the music died, leaving a ringing in his ears.

"Hey," he hissed. "Turn Adam back on."

The edge of his bed dipped. Expecting Natasha, since she'd made it a habit to check in on him daily, he rolled over onto his back only to blink up at the concerned face of his mother.

"Mom," he mumbled. "What are you doing here?"

"I should have checked on you sooner," his mother said, a pout in her voice. "You have your sister to thank for keeping me away. Since the fall lines are out today, she's off to New York for some shopping, so she finally allowed me in here. I swear that girl takes after me."

"That she does." A lightness he hadn't felt in a while blossomed in his chest. He'd missed his mother more than he cared to admit.

"Are you seriously going to spend the entire day in bed?" She began rubbing up and down his arm over the covers. "It's already way past lunch. I actually think the sun is beginning to set."

"I know what you're trying to do," he grumbled. He had that tasting with Mrs. Grant. He couldn't cancel, seeing as the event was in two days.

"And what is that?"

Her question sounded way too innocent. "You're reminding me that there are things I have to do."

"Well, Eleanor did call to confirm, so I thought it best to get you. Plus, aren't you tired of listening to that album over and over again? I practically have the lyrics of every song memorized. And your father sent me here to beg you to spare his ears from bleeding by at least considering switching to another band. Springsteen, perhaps?"

In exasperation, Nathan stuck his arms out of the covers, effectively folding the duvet away from the upper half of his body. "Can I just stay in bed forever? I can play the role of your invalid son."

"As much as I love *The Secret Garden*, you know I can't let you do that."

"Oh, well. At least I tried."

The way she crossed her arms and frowned was like looking

in the mirror, except at someone twenty years older. "Tash filled me in on everything, and I honestly don't understand why you're allowing this to happen. I thought you loved Preston."

At her eyebrow arch, he shoved his fingers through his hair and groaned. "Of course I love him. He's the one. And that's the reason why I'm here."

"Hmmm . . ." She tapped her foot against his nightstand, a faraway look in her eyes. "Then tell me your side of the story. I know what Tash told me, but I want to hear it from you. What happened?"

"Long story short?" His brow furrowed. "Preston is living his dream at the Bennett Club."

"You don't need to sacrifice love just because you have a dream."

"Mom, swimming will always be his priority. The fact that he'd forgotten we were going on our first real date is a testament to that. And there's nothing I can say that won't make me look selfish. As much as I wanted him to stay, I knew I couldn't say anything."

"That boy." She shook her head. "Always has swimming on the brain."

"It's that commitment I love about him most," Nathan whispered.

"Then what are you still doing here?" His mother's smile held a hint of mischief. "I honestly think you should get on the next plane to Colorado and make him see reason."

"Mom!" he whined. "I can't do that."

"And why not?"

"I will never allow myself to stand in the way of his future."

"Looks to me like you're holding yourself back." She patted his arm.

He sat up and threw the stifling covers aside. Then he scrambled out of bed and went straight to the bathroom.

"I come to check on you and suddenly you want out of bed?" his mother asked.

Shirtless, Nathan leaned out of the bathroom to narrow his gaze at her. "Thanks for reminding me that I have my own dream to focus on."

Her smile went from impish to megawatt. "I get that, but it doesn't mean you two can't work things out."

Nathan thought about it for a second. "This doesn't change anything. I'm going to work."

An hour later, he pushed the conversation he'd had with his mother to the farthest reaches of his mind. Party planning was his life now. If he had lost his chance at love, then by the grace of everything holy in his world, he would be the best goddamn party planner even if it killed him. And all that started with pulling off the luncheon without a hitch, starting with the soul-sucking tasting.

Eleanor Grant was living up to her party-planner-nightmare reputation. As if the constant e-mails and calls during Nathan and Preston's trip weren't bad enough, now that Nathan was back, she insisted on calling him about every little detail. Like tapers. Even if the occasion was to be held during the lunch hour, she insisted on tapers. And not just any old tapers either. The candles needed to be cream and cut to eight inches. There were seven-inch tapers and nine-inch tapers. But she wanted eight inches—no more and no less. So Nathan and Didi spent his entire second night back at Dodge Cove cutting candlesticks. She was such a great assistant, never complaining and happily jumping into each new task. He loved her even more for it.

Also, the drapes had to match the table linens. Even the napkins had to match. When he presented Eleanor with the neutral color options such as off-white, ivory, and cream, she shot them all down, asking for eggshell. This was pretty easy, since he knew of a store that carried the linens in that particular shade. Feeling accomplished, he'd shown her the linens, and she insisted they weren't what eggshell looked like. Ready to pull his hair out, he kept trying until he realized what Mrs. Grant had really wanted were cream linens to match the candlesticks and drapes.

To say the entire time he'd been back had been torture would be putting things mildly. It did get his mind off more painful thoughts, so he couldn't complain. Much. All Mrs. Grant had to finalize was the food. Thank goodness the entertainment had been booked in advance and the venue was ready.

Easing his death grip on his tablet for fear of cracking the screen, Nathan took a deep breath and said, "We have a selection of three soups to start."

At his signal, the server placed three bowls from the china selection for the occasion in front of Mrs. Grant in her regal Chanel suit.

"First we have a savory beet soup in this fantastic magenta," he continued, indicating the first bowl. "The color is as eye-catching as it is appetizing."

Eyebrow raised, she picked up her silver spoon. Nathan gritted his teeth through her three-pronged tasting process. The first taste was to prepare the palate. The second was to acclimate the palate. And the third was the actual tasting of the food. Not savoring. Oh no. This was tasting in its finest form. Tedious, but what else did Nathan have to do that day?

"Too tart," she said after putting down the spoon.

Maintaining a neutral tone, he indicated the next bowl. "For the next offering, our chef has prepared a creamy carrot soup, which I believe you will find delightful."

"Nathan," she snipped, her spine ramrod straight. "If I want your opinion, I will certainly ask for it."

He mumbled an apology, which sadly ended in an unintended curse word.

"Excuse me?" Eleanor shifted in her seat so she could look over at him.

Nathan faked a sneeze. "I apologize. I must be coming down with something."

"Better not be getting sick. I wouldn't want you to be absent during the day of."

God forbid. His reputation was on the line.

Professional. He must remain professional. The recommendation hung in the balance. He just kept reminding himself that she was Preston's mother. Nathan had no right to be rude to Preston's mother.

"Too sweet," Mrs. Grant said after tasting the carrot soup.

Praying to anyone who would listen that the third soup would do the trick, because he didn't have any other options without having the chef cook them first, Nathan indicated the last bowl with a wave of his hand. But before he could mention the name of the dish, the woman he'd sold his soul to for this event spoke first.

"I had a chat with my son this morning," she began in her usual clipped tone as she made notes on the pad to her right.

He bit the inside of his cheek to keep from speaking. Asking how Preston was had been a habit when they were apart for a long period of time. Which wasn't often. In fact, this was the longest they had gone without speaking in years. Preston hadn't called like he said he would. And Nathan hadn't wanted to dial his number for fear of breaking into tears while they spoke.

At his silence, she continued, "I have to be honest. While I don't completely understand your life choices, I do know one thing." She paused, the tip of her pen hovering over the pad. "You are good for my son."

"I'm sorry?" Nathan blurted out, unsure if he had heard her correctly.

When Eleanor sighed, it was the smallest slip of breath. She put down her pen and waved him over until he stood to her left. She shifted in her seat once again and looked up at him with a stern expression. In the back of Nathan's mind, he knew the woman before him would be stunning if her brow wasn't set in that permanent scowl. Maybe if she smiled more.

He was pulled back to the present when she said, "As you know, I am not the most affectionate of mothers."

Nathan had to bite his tongue to hold in the confirmation of her statement. The last thing he wanted was to anger the dragon unnecessarily. He waited instead.

"And speaking to my son has always been a formal affair," she went on. "But this morning . . ."

When she shook her head, Nathan feared she wouldn't continue. He held his breath until his lungs hurt. Good thing she spoke again before he passed out.

"This morning he didn't seem himself, and I have to wonder why."

Not himself? Nathan's heart squeezed. He really wanted to ask, but before he could, she beat him to it.

"So whatever it is that has happened between you and my son, fix it."

Her tone was so commanding that Nathan almost said he would. But it wasn't his place to fix things that he hadn't broken. So instead he said he would think about it and moved on to the last soup choice.

Twenty-Five

PRESTON PLOWED THROUGH the water like a man possessed, but he no longer felt like he was flying. It seemed as if each molecule surrounding his skin was infused with pain and stress instead of the usual soothing relaxation.

He couldn't shake the nagging feeling that he had forgotten something. That he was supposed to do something. But as soon as he'd arrived at the Bennett Club facility, Coach Bennett put him to work right away. Swimming had become his life more than it had ever been. He ate, breathed, dreamed, and thought about nothing else. Yet at the back of his mind there was an itch he couldn't seem to scratch.

Anger and frustration propelled him forward in the final few meters. His hands slapped against the tile. The sound used to send a zing of accomplishment through him. Now it merely served as a reminder that he'd reached his goal.

Immediately he planted his feet and pulled off his cap and goggles. He looked up at the assistant coach assigned to all the newbies. For a moment, a different face stared back at him. One with bright blue eyes and a winning smile.

To clear the image, blaming it on the stinging chlorine, he wiped a hand down his face and blinked several times. Maybe the lack of sleep was catching up with him. He still hadn't recovered from the jet lag, despite the Ambien he'd taken on the plane ride almost ten days ago.

"Looking good, Pres!" The assistant coach glanced at the stopwatch, then at the tablet that contained swimming stats. "You actually shaved a tenth of a second from your time. Not at the level of your tryouts just yet, but getting there. Keep this up and you'll be a beast come the qualifiers next year."

A tenth of a second. That was the amount of time it took to change his life, but was it a life he still wanted?

Of course.

What the hell was he thinking? He shoved the cap and goggles back on.

"I'm going again," he said, already pushing up and out of the pool to take his place on the starting block.

"Actually . . ." The assistant paused.

"What?"

The guy hiked his thumb toward the bleachers. "Someone's been waiting for you. Go catch up and we'll pick this up later this afternoon."

With hope surging in his chest, Preston whipped his head

in the direction the coach indicated. His gaze immediately settled on familiar dark hair and blue eyes, but the similarities ended there. His heart plummeted for some reason. Of course it wouldn't be Nathan. He was probably back in DoCo finalizing plans for his mother's luncheon. Why would he expect anything less?

Caleb stood from the fifth row and gave him a small wave.

Shoulders slumping, he padded to the bottom of the bleacher steps as Caleb climbed down to meet him.

"Aww!" Caleb said, giving him a couple of soft slaps on the cheek. "Look at that face."

Preston grunted. "I'm not making a face."

"How far the stoic has fallen." Caleb tsked. "You should really hide your disappointment better, buddy."

"Who says I'm disappointed?" Preston asked in his usual monotone, schooling his face into what he hoped was an expressionless mask.

"I think you're forgetting that we grew up together." Caleb crossed his arms and widened his stance. "You can't fool me, so don't even bother trying."

"I hate to be rude . . ." He pulled off his cap and goggles again. Water still dripped from his arms and chest.

"Whoa! You shaved your head!" Caleb gasped, preventing Preston from asking his question.

Automatically Preston reached up and rubbed his palm over the buzz cut. "It's nothing."

"It actually looks good. Maybe I should get a buzz cut too."

"What the hell are you doing here, Caleb?" Preston finally got to ask. He had to admit that seeing Caleb again did bring a measure of comfort. Being in Colorado alone was lonely. He missed . . . his life in Dodge Cove.

"Just thought we could talk," Caleb said way too innocently.

Preston's brow furrowed. "Don't think I don't recognize that casual shrug of yours. After all, we did grow up together. You're up to something."

"So what if I am?" Caleb challenged, his gaze hardening to sapphires.

"I'm really busy." Preston turned around, heading toward the showers.

"He's been blasting *Songs About Jane* since he got back," Caleb called after him, his voice bouncing off the facility's walls.

Preston froze in his tracks. *Songs About Jane* was Nathan's go-to heartbreak album. He only played it on full blast if it was all systems down. Last time that happened Adam Levine had announced he was getting married.

He turned around. "Is he okay?"

The smug look on Caleb's face said it all. "I'm starving. Where's a good place to eat around here?"

Preston led the way into a family-owned restaurant that served pretty decent food. Since he'd only been in Colorado a short time, he hadn't had time to really explore the area surrounding the Bennett Club. Mostly he ate what the nutritionist prepared at the facility and stayed at the dorms after practice.

Caleb followed him in as a server approached. She greeted them with a smile and indicated one of the back booths. Preston gave her a nod and headed for the booth as the smell of bacon grease and sizzling burgers wafted from behind the counter.

Once seated, they looked over the menu, which showed pretty standard diner fare, and gave their orders. A burger and fries for the both of them.

"I'm sorry I couldn't bring you to somewhere fancier," Preston said when the woman left to fetch their drinks.

"I'm used to it. Didi's been dragging me to every fast-food place and diner in Dodge Cove."

"How is she?" Preston asked. He had a soft spot for Caleb's girlfriend and maintained that he'd had a hand in bringing them together.

A silly grin spread across the Parker cousin's face. "She's magnificent. She's actually helping Nathan out with the luncheon."

Preston's eyebrows lifted. "Nathan? Having an assistant? That's new." Then he sobered. "Not that I'm not happy to see you, but why are you here? Why is Nathan blasting *Songs About Jane*?"

"Once upon a time you were a voice of reason when I thought all hope was lost with Didi. I'm here to return that favor." Caleb looked him dead in the eye, a crooked grin on his lips. "You know, there is a way to determine if you love someone. Do you want to try it?"

"What does *it* entail?" Preston asked suspiciously.

"You just have to answer the first thing that comes to mind when I start asking you questions. It's actually this *Cosmo* quiz Didi made me take."

"I'm not taking a fucking *Cosmo* quiz!" Preston said, scandalized.

"Come on. It works. Trust me."

Still skeptical, Preston stomped down his embarrassment as

best he could. No harm in answering a few questions. Right? He looked around to make sure no one was listening in on them before he nodded, hands on his knees.

Caleb lifted a finger. "Question one. Who is the first person you think about the second you wake up?"

"Nathan." No joke. The second Preston opened his eyes, he'd wonder what Nathan was doing that very moment. More so now after their trip.

"All right. Second question. Who is the last person you think about before you go to sleep at night?"

"Nathan." Preston kept reminding himself to send Nathan a text or to call, but at the end of each practice day he was so exhausted that all he could do was sleep.

"Good." Caleb nodded once. "Third question. Who is the first person you'd want to tell when something good happens?"

"Nathan," Preston whispered, thinking back. Yes. Every time something good happened in his life, he wanted Nathan to be the first to know. More so than his parents. In everything, the one constant was Nathan.

"Fourth question." Caleb's previous smugness returned. "When you need help or have a problem, who is the person you go to?"

The answer was simple for two reasons. If he didn't tell Nathan, then he would be risking great bodily harm. And the other was it seemed his childhood friend had all the answers. When Preston was injured, Nathan had been the one who helped him the most. When he needed a distraction from thinking about the results of the tryouts, Nathan had suggested the trip. Granted, things imploded most of the time, but Preston didn't regret going.

"Last question."

"Do we have to?" Preston already knew where this was going.

"Just one more." Caleb winked. "And when you close your eyes and think of your seventy-year-old self, who is the one you want holding your hand?"

"Damn it!"

"Why did you walk out on Nathan when you two were supposed to go on a date?"

The question blindsided him. For a few seconds all he could really do was concentrate on breathing. Thank God they were already seated, because he'd lost feeling in his legs.

"Jesus." He wiped his face with both hands. "I completely fucked up."

"Explain."

As if he was punched back to life, the words came spilling out. "When we got back to the hotel, I got the e-mail about getting into the Bennett Club. I was so excited that I completely forgot about our date. I'm such an asshole." It all started to make sense. "No wonder Nathan was acting weird after I told him I was leaving. Fuck!" Preston eased out of the booth.

"Whoa!" Caleb went after him. "Where do you think you're going?"

Preston turned back around and glared, nostrils flaring.

"Stop freaking out." The smile Caleb gave him showed his triumph. "I already have us booked on the red-eye out of Denver tonight. I figure that way you have a chance to make up an excuse to your coach."

"Has anyone ever told you how scary you can get when you

have your mind set on something?" Preston asked lightly, all the burdens weighing down his shoulders easing.

"Not since yesterday." Caleb ushered his friend back to the booth. "Plus, you can't just go there without a plan."

"I'm guessing you already have one in mind?" Preston was feeling slightly light-headed when he returned to his side of the booth.

"I may have a couple of suggestions," Caleb said, a dangerous twinkle in his eye. "But sweeping Nate off his feet should come from you. I'm just here to help in any way that I can."

"Let's eat first." Preston waved for the server again. A burger and fries just wouldn't cut it. "I do my best thinking on a full stomach."

Twenty-Six

THE DODGE COVE Solarium was both the best and worst venue for the Society of Dodge Cove Matrons luncheon. Nathan blamed the suggestion in his last-minute proposal on the delirium of the fever he'd suffered in Rome. Ideas and reality were totally different animals.

It was the best because of its stunning views of the DoCo Botanical Gardens. The walls and ceiling were made of glass, with maple wood paneling. Inside it had potted fruit trees and a selection of blooming plants. Quaint without being overbearing.

In contrast, it was the worst location because the entire structure was made of glass. For lunch, that meant the noonday sun beating down on all of them could turn the place into an oven. Second was its size. Nathan kept insisting that they couldn't fit tables for eight, let alone for twelve, inside. But Eleanor Grant was implacable once she had made up her mind. In her own words, she would have the luncheon at the solarium if she had to buy the entire Botanical Gardens to do it. Considering how vast the Grant holdings were, she could make good on her threat in a heartbeat.

So, after making several calls, most of them to the fire marshal, and a little creative maneuvering with the help of Didi, they managed to fit six tables for twelve inside the octagonal space. It was probably one of the hardest things Nathan had had to do for an event.

Besides the tables, they needed space for a podium. As per Mrs. Grant's instructions, it had to be on an elevated platform. Which meant Nathan had to have one built from scratch. Because of everything they had to cram into the space, the poor caterer would have to serve the food from outside. As a concession, Nathan had a special tent built for the chef and his crew, complete with air-conditioning should the sun decide it wanted to be hot that day.

Then there were the drapes that Eleanor insisted on. The solarium wasn't made to hold curtains. It was built to showcase panoramic views of the gardens. Once again he had to use all his God-given creativity, since they couldn't make any changes to the structure. Adding curtain rods was a huge no-no. At the last minute he found a way to maneuver around drilling hooks in the walls by hanging the fabric along the wooden beams. Nearly gave him a stroke at the age of eighteen, but by the holy grace of fashion he had managed it.

Come event day, the solarium was bustling with activity.

He'd arrived early to inspect the space. The servers had draped all the linens and were already assembling the place settings when the flowers arrived.

Everything was a well-orchestrated performance. Nathan had planned each detail down to the takedown of their setup after the event. The solarium would be back to its original condition at exactly four in the afternoon that day.

He checked the time on his tablet after he'd signed for the flowers. Didi was directing the servers where to place the arrangements. Not a minute later, Mrs. Grant appeared by his side in an impeccable white suit—Chanel, of course. Several strands of pearls dangled from her neck, the longest of which reached the waistband of her pencil skirt. Her blond hair was elegantly arranged—not a lock out of place. And she smelled of lilacs.

"Mrs. Grant," he greeted her, giving her a kiss on each cheek. "You look absolutely divine."

"I trust that everything is in order" was her ever-curt response.

Nathan had made the mistake of calling her Eleanor once. She'd put him in his place in ten seconds flat. Sometimes he couldn't fathom how such a frightening woman could have produced such a wonderful son. Well, considering Preston's unyielding sense of focus to the point where he would forget a date because of an important e-mail, Nathan completely understood.

Mentally slapping himself for thinking of *him*, he forced himself to focus on the job at hand. He would not be able to breathe easy until this event was over. The planning had certainly shaved years off his life, that was for sure.

"I want all the courses served at seventeen-minute intervals,"

Mrs. Grant said as she scanned the area where the lunch would be held. No doubt she was eyeballing the length of the tapers.

"I will let the chef and servers know," he replied, making a note of it on his tablet. "What if the matrons aren't finished—"

"You will clear and serve the next course in exactly seventeen minutes," she interrupted, her tone final.

"Seventeen minutes it is." Nathan took a deep, hopefully calming breath. He was surprised he hadn't developed a stomach ulcer during the entire planning stage. He constantly had to remind himself that the recommendation afterward would be worth it. This luncheon would be in the local paper and every party-planning blog come morning.

As the Grant matriarch gave him last-minute instructions, he vowed to never again plan an event for her. He would rather poke an eyeball out first.

Already a headache threatened to pulse between his temples. The servers gave him sympathetic glances as they passed to accomplish whatever task they had been assigned. They knew his pain. When he had set out to slay his dragon, he'd never thought it would be this challenging. He finally understood what drove those other planners toward mental breakdowns.

When Mrs. Grant finally left him to harass someone else, Nathan gave in to massaging his forehead. Almost immediately Didi appeared with a glass of water and an Advil. He thanked her profusely and swallowed the tablet.

Taking another steadying breath, he left the solarium to give the chef his new instructions.

Exactly an hour later, the matrons started arriving. The gasps and exclamations of wonder warmed his heart as he stood by the entrance, greeting each and every one of them.

Mrs. Grant was inside, helping seat her guests. He had said she didn't have to, but Preston's mother was immovable. Just like her son.

As if on cue, the walls of his chest contracted. Just thinking of him was debilitating.

As he fought to keep a smile on his face, he wondered how long the seemingly fathomless aching would last. And if he would survive it. He'd never believed it was possible to die of a broken heart, but considering the amount of pain he was in, he might as well be a dead man standing.

He was in the middle of greeting Mrs. Hassleback when something green drove past in his periphery. They weren't far from the entrance to the botanical gardens, so from where he stood, he could see the cars driving by to let their passengers out. He looked past the oil tycoon's widow. The instant he recognized the Wrangler, he thought his heart would stop beating.

Seconds later the driver's door opened, and a long leg he would recognize anywhere stretched out. Nathan's breath hitched. It couldn't be. No. It couldn't possibly be *him*. But he knew in his heart of hearts that only one person in DoCo drove a Jeep like that.

Preston stepped out of the driver's side, his hair in a tight buzz cut.

Nathan stopped breathing altogether. If he'd thought Preston looked good with long hair, the buzz cut gave him an edge that pushed him into a hot scale that hadn't been invented yet.

It took everything in Nathan not to make a run for it. Whether it was toward the boy he loved or away, he couldn't quite tell. Then all his awe disappeared when he spotted his cousin trailing after the swimmer.

So that was where Caleb had disappeared to.

Nathan used the spark of anger to unstick his feet from the ground. He hurried toward the pair. Despite the joy he felt at seeing Preston again, his resolve remained intact. *The guy shouldn't be in DoCo*, Nathan thought.

"I would ask what you are doing here, but looking at the unrepentant glee on my cousin's face already tells me the answer," he hissed. "Actually, I don't want to know."

Preston paused, just looking at him silently through the classic Ray-Bans he wore. Nathan owned a similar pair. They had bought them together just that summer. *Ugh*. He looked too delicious for words. Not ready to let go of his ire, Nathan shifted all his attention to Caleb.

"You!" He pointed at his cousin, who didn't even have the decency to flinch. "Don't think I don't know what you're up to by bringing him here."

"Oh?" Caleb raised an eyebrow at him. "And what exactly am I up to?"

Nathan didn't have a chance to respond. In seconds he was engulfed by the most powerful arms he had ever known—capable of slaying all who dared to challenge him in the pool. He all but melted the second his face was crushed against that unyielding chest and he inhaled the scent of chlorine and soap he'd craved during the darkest, loneliest hours of the night.

"I'm so sorry," Preston whispered. "I fucked up."

A shudder ran through Nathan as that deep, rich voice that teased of secret encounters in dark corners reached his ear. A part of him wanted to forget everything and just kiss Preston senseless right there. But the more responsible part, the one that had watched him train for endless hours every day, knew Dodge Cove wasn't the place for the swimmer.

It took all the willpower he could muster, but Nathan eventually managed to step away from the embrace. Once he was breathing fresh air again, he was able to think more clearly.

"Whatever it is you think you're doing, don't bother," he said, rejoicing inside that his voice didn't falter. "There's nothing for you here."

"Nathan——" Caleb began.

Preston's raised hand cut off the rest of what his cousin had been about to say. He removed his sunglasses and deliberately took the time to fold and hook them against the collar of his white T-shirt. Then he rubbed a hand over his short hair, which Nathan couldn't stop staring at.

"I know where I should be," Preston said with a firm resolve in his voice that was surely inherited from his mother. "You don't have to worry about Coach Bennett. He knows I'm here. In fact, he only gave me a couple of days. Then it's back to Colorado."

"I say leave now and don't look back." Even as Nathan spoke the words, he knew he would be lying to himself if he didn't admit that he was happy to have a couple more days with Preston.

"I'll leave as soon as I finish what I came here to do."

"And what is that?"

Preston reached out a hand for him. "Come with me and see."

As if he was under some kind of mind control, Nathan immediately lifted his hand with the purpose of entwining their fingers. But before their palms could touch, he remembered what day it was. He pulled back and indicated the solarium.

"As you can see, I have an event to run," he said. "I don't have time to leave with you."

It was for the best. Leaving would just get him into so much trouble. He'd already accepted that he had no place in Preston's heart. Nothing could change that.

"That's what I'm here for," Didi said. She took the tablet from his hands and flitted away when he made a grab for it. "I'm sure you already have everything set. All I have to do is supervise."

"And I'll make sure to help her," Caleb piped up, looking too smug for his own good.

"If this was any other event, I would be happy to let you take over," Nathan said to Didi. Then he placed his hands on his hips and turned to scowl at Preston. "You know your mother would not accept me leaving an event I'd planned for her. What would she think?"

"I think you should go with my son," came the stern voice from behind him.

Slowly, Nathan turned around to face the cool expression on Mrs. Grant's face. She shifted her hazel eyes toward her son, and the corners of her lips pushed up in the smallest smile ever known to man.

"Hello, Preston," she said.

"Mother," Preston answered, but Nathan had his back to him so he couldn't tell what expression Preston had on.

"We will be discussing what you have done with your hair later." Then she returned her steely gaze back to meet what Nathan hoped was a pleading one. "You have done an excellent job here, Nathan. Consider that recommendation yours."

He was stunned. That was the best compliment he ever could have gotten from the woman who ate party planners for breakfast. He had done it. He had slain his dragon.

"I believe Didi is capable enough to take over. She has been an excellent liaison while you were in Europe. I wondered why you hadn't hired her sooner," she continued. "Now, my son traveled a long way to be here today. Do I have to fire you to get you to leave with him?"

Nathan swallowed and shook his head.

"Good." She nodded once, clasping her hands together. "Now go before I change my mind."

Twenty-Seven

NATHAN SAT IN the passenger seat of Preston's Wrangler in stunned silence. His shock was left over from what had happened at the solarium. Ten minutes must have passed since they had driven away.

This was a first. It seemed as if they had all ganged up on him. The plan was surely Caleb and Didi's doing, but to have Mrs. Grant actually kick him out of the luncheon he had patiently put together for her? Surely she wasn't in cahoots with them. Did anyone still say *cahoots* anymore?

Trying to act calm had only lasted for about the first mile. Since then he'd been tapping his fingers and looking out the window. Normally it would be him planning the scheme or actually helping enact it. To be on the receiving end was surreal.

"Don't think I don't know what you're up to," he said,

resting his chin on the heel of his hand as he watched the scenery zoom past.

"Oh?" his driver asked, uncharacteristic mischief in his tone. "Tell me, what exactly am I up to?"

Honestly? Nathan had no idea. His brain wouldn't engage long enough for him to figure out the possibilities. He was too aware of the hotness sitting within reach. His lips twitched for a kiss.

Seriously, he had to stop these useless lustful thoughts. Preston would only be in DoCo for a couple of days. He wasn't prepared for the kind of heartbreak that would follow having to watch him leave a second time.

"You shaved your head," he mumbled instead.

"Coach wants us to simulate competition conditions at all times. So no more hair for a while. I was afraid he would even take my eyebrows. You don't like it?"

Nathan would have laughed if the butterflies weren't performing an entire gymnastics routine in his stomach. He knew Preston had always shaved before every competition. At least their high school swimming coach had let him keep his hair. Bennett must be old-school.

"Wasn't actually thinking that, but now that you put it out there . . ." Nathan slanted a glance at the boy, who once again ran his hand over the strands cut close to his skull.

"Fuck." Preston chuckled. "I have a feeling you're holding back your opinion to spare my feelings."

Heat climbed up from Nathan's neck to find a home across his cheeks and the bridge of his nose. If he didn't know any better, he'd think Preston was teasing him on purpose. For the sake of his sanity and both their hearts, he had to steer the conversation back to reality.

"Look, I really don't think this is a good idea," he said after clearing his too-tight throat. He could already feel the corners of his eyes stinging. He wanted his *Songs About Jane* and he wanted it now. "Why don't you just drop me off at my house and you can do whatever it is you came back to do by yourself?"

"Uh, I can't do that."

Nathan turned his head so he faced Preston fully. "And why is that?"

"Because what I need to do involves you."

If Nathan had thought he couldn't blush anymore, those words brought all the remaining blood in his body rushing to his head. The swimmer didn't even look like he was kidding. He just kept his eyes on the road.

"Pres . . ." Nathan paused when he realized where they were going. "You're taking me to your house?"

Preston made the turn into the massive estate's gravel drive-way. Fully grown pine trees flanked them on both sides like silent sentinels standing guard against intruders. As always the manor was a breathtaking sight.

The Jeep eased to a smooth stop in front of it, and Preston cut the engine.

"Come on." He unsnapped his seat belt and got out.

Nathan did the same and asked, "What are we doing here?"

His kidnapper reached out for him. He hesitated. And then, just like in Venice, Preston said, "You're overthinking it. Just take my hand, Nate."

It was completely ridiculous, but the words touched Nathan to the core. Speechless, he took Preston's hand and let him lead the way into the woods. From the confidence in Preston's stride, Nathan could tell he knew where they were going. He gave himself over to whatever the plan was. He figured, what did he have to lose? He'd already had his heart broken once and survived.

With the sun still high in the sky, golden spears burst through the branches of the trees. They had played in these woods as children, so walking between the giants wasn't intimidating at all. When they reached the small clearing, Nathan's eyes widened.

Blankets and pillows were artfully arranged into a comfortable nest beneath the tallest tree in their Fort of Solitude. Fat candles in protective glass containers were lit everywhere. The soft glow of their light created an inviting space. Rose petals were sprinkled all over the entire area.

"I hope the rose petals weren't overkill. Didi said you'd like them," Preston said, a slight hesitation in his tone.

Nathan gasped. "You did this for me?"

The awe in Nathan's voice filled Preston's heart with so much joy he thought it would explode. He bowed his head in an attempt to hide his blush as he said, "This was the place where you convinced me not to give up. I hope that I can do the same for you now. Tell me if I get this right." He positioned himself in front of Nathan and cleared his throat before he continued. " 'For my whole life, we never crossed the line. Only friends in my mind, but now I realize . . . It was always you.' "

Like a freight train without brakes, unstoppable tears welled in Nathan's eyes and spilled over the brim to stream down his cheeks.

"Wait. What the fuck's happening? Why are you crying?"

"You're not seriously quoting a Maroon 5 song at me right now." The last word Nathan spoke turned into a sob that ended in a sniff.

Preston's brow crumpled. He bent down so they were at eye level. "And that's a bad thing? I thought they were your favorite band."

In annoyance, Nathan swiped at his tearstained cheeks. "You know they are."

Still unable to understand completely, Preston ran his hand over the top of his head until he reached the back of his neck. He squeezed at the tension building in the muscles there. "Then why the tears? Don't tell me I'm fucking this up too? My ego just can't take it."

Like a sudden drought taking away all available moisture from the ground, Nathan's tears dried up. With a last sniff, he said, "No. No. You're not fucking it up."

Preston's sigh came and went. He closed his eyes for the briefest second to gather his thoughts. When he was sure he knew what he wanted to say, he said, "Like the song says, it's always been you, Nate. I hate myself for being so blind."

Because of their height difference, Nathan was forced to look up at him. Not that Preston minded. It gave him the best view of those watery blue eyes. They reminded him of the pool.

He had always thought that nothing could replace swimming in his heart. That when he swam back toward the starting block to win a race, it was a homecoming. But what he had come to realize was that the person who always stood by that block with a stopwatch in his hand was Nathan. He wasn't swimming home to win. He was swimming home to *him*.

Preston bent down and kissed Nathan. It took a moment for Nathan to respond, but when he did, Preston felt it like a wave crashing into shore: all at once, with arms thrown around his neck. But before the kiss could go any further, he reached for Nathan's wrists and disentangled his hold.

The look of disappointment in Nathan's eyes was as devastating as his previous distress. As much as Preston wanted to soothe him with more kisses, there were important words that still needed to be said. He reached inside his pocket and produced the item he had been carrying around since Amsterdam.

"My love lock," Nathan said, eyes widening in surprise. "I thought I'd lost it."

Preston showed him the side with their initials carved on it. "I have to admit that I didn't understand why you were so angry about the love locks when we were in Paris, but when I saw the initials that night you told me you loved me—"

"Which I still insist was the worst way to ever tell someone that you have feelings for them," came the interruption.

Chuckling, Preston continued. "Seeing this lock was what made me realize that despite the effects of the pot brownie— or maybe I should say because of it—you were telling the truth, and I felt the same way for you. I actually planned on telling you in Venice."

"The date!"

Preston nodded. "I shouldn't have walked away that night. I should have taken you on that date. We could have celebrated me getting into the Bennett Club. Instead I let my excitement take over, forgetting your feelings."

"But I get it now. You leaving was the right thing. Why are you shaking your head?"

"Because Caleb made me see that pursuing my dream isn't enough."

"I don't understand."

"Nate," Preston whispered, taking his hand. "Don't you see? It's not a dream without you there with me."

"Pres," Nathan said. It sounded more like a sigh.

"No." Preston's grip tightened. "I'm not letting you talk me out of this. I love you too much to lose you."

Nathan stared up at him in awe.

Preston planted a kiss on the back of Nathan's hand. "I don't have a single memory that doesn't have you in it. And I can't imagine creating new ones without you. I love you, Nathan Parker. I wouldn't be the man I am today if it wasn't for you."

In response, Nathan took the lock. "You win."

Preston's eyebrow arched. "And what exactly did I win?"

"Most romantic confession ever. I didn't think you had it in you. No offense."

"None taken." He pulled Nathan closer and whispered against his mouth, "Thank you."

"For what?"

"For taking me to Europe. For showing me there's more to life than just training to achieve my dream."

Meeting Nathan's gaze, Preston bent down and resumed their kiss. His heart pounded for a whole different reason. Without breaking the kiss, he turned them around and gently nudged Nathan down until he was lying on his back on top of the blankets.

With each button Preston opened down Nathan's shirt, he placed an openmouthed kiss along the column of his neck. Nathan sighed. The feel of Nathan's body beneath him spread a sense of security in Preston despite his shaking hands and fumbling fingers. He gave himself over to the sensations that being honest with his feelings brought out with each intimate touch. All of the most important words had already been said. This time was for a different kind of conversation. One spoken through moans and loving caresses.

Hours later Nathan eased out of Preston's sleep embrace and made his way to the ridge that faced the man-made lake below them. As daylight slowly gave way to the coming night, the sky was awash with the golden-orange colors of sunset. He took in a deep breath as if for the first time and smiled at the brand-new beginning.

"Aren't you cold?" came the whisper from behind him.

Seconds later, strong arms that never failed to make him feel safe wrapped around him and pulled him into an equally powerful chest. He went willingly, the blanket they'd used cocooning him in welcome warmth.

"Not anymore." Nathan laced his fingers through the large hands that touched him so gently, almost reverently. Each caress conveyed devotion to the highest degree.

"What are you thinking about?" Preston whispered into his ear. Not hours ago that same deep voice had called out his name during the most beautiful expression of love between two people.

"Something's been bothering me since you left for Colorado."

"Oh?"

"Where have you been living?"

"The facility dorms," Preston said as the sun reached the mountain wall in its descent.

"Oh no! No, no, no, no, no." Nathan clucked his tongue. "The dorms just won't do. I'll make sure to find us an apartment when we get there."

"We?"

He turned in the circle of Preston's arms and looked up into the face he knew in his heart he would grow old with. "Yes, we. You didn't think after that stunning confession that I would ever consider trying the long-distance thing, did you?"

"But what about your party planning?"

"Silly swimmer, with your mother's recommendation, I can set up shop *anywhere*."

"Oh. Well then . . ." Preston pressed a kiss against Nathan's forehead before he ran the tip of his nose down the bridge of Nathan's and kissed his lips briefly, sweetly.

"Let's go home," Nathan said with a playful nudge. "We have lots of planning to do before you have to leave."

"Planning?" Preston asked.

"Don't start," Nathan warned.

"Hey, as long as you follow me there as soon as you can, I'd sleep on a bench if I had to."

"Bench. *Pshaw!*" Nathan squeezed Preston's chin. "Get ready, Preston Ulysses Grant, because I'm pulling out all the stops."

"Oh yeah?" Preston grinned, taking Nathan's hand and lacing their fingers together.

A smile that came from a well overflowing with love blossomed on Nathan's face. "Yeah . . . because I've just decided that from now on there's no holding back."

ACKNOWLEDGMENTS

NATHAN AND PRESTON'S story wouldn't have come about without the love and support of so many people.

My mother is my rock. She is the strongest person I know. And she is the one who taught me how to love unconditionally. Without her, I wouldn't be here literally, figuratively, emotionally, and whatever else. Thank you, Momager. You are amazing.

Holly, thank you for continuing to challenge and believe in me. I wouldn't be the writer I am today without your editorial letters, Track Changes comments, and e-mails. All the answered e-mails. They mean so much to me. I always look forward to our Google Hangout chats. Thank you for making magic happen!

Lauren, thank you for helping me bring out Preston's voice. Our boy was so quiet I wouldn't have heard him over Nathan's fabulous chattering without your on-point direction. You are priceless.

To everyone at Swoon Reads HQ who believed in me enough to green-light *No Holding Back* and *No Second Chances*. I am forever grateful. Thank you for making so many dreams come true—not only for me, but for all the writers you have taken under your wing. Thank you for allowing me to share Preston and Nathan's story with the world. We need more of their love out there.

To all my Swoon Sisters. You ladies are magnificent. I couldn't be prouder to be part of such an illustrious group. Each and every one of your books inspires me deeply. Thank you for doing what you do.

To Noey, Pam, and Rika, thank you for just being you. We might not talk often. We might only see each other when the planets align, but your presence in my life saves me in more ways than I can express in words.

To the great Mina Esguerra. What you do for writers is selfless. Your unfailing support for everyone's success continues to amaze me. Keep up the great work. *hugs*

To Jerzon, Gavin, Erika Joy, Jas, Camelle, Rafael, Jerby, Fay, Inah, thank you for your continued support! I know I missed a ton of people, but I wouldn't be here today without you. Thank you for making me laugh. Thank you for tagging me on every cat-related post on Facebook. Thank you for coming to see me at signings. My world is so much better with you in it. Be kind, always.

Kai, this is it, girl! For the love of BL. For all the fandoms. For all the OTPs. And all the yaoi in the world. Preston and Nathan love you.

Anne Plaza, my Sailor Moon sister. Keep writing, sis! You are a-mazing. Next time you have to take me with you when you decide to go to Singapore.

To all the #StrangeLit writers. You inspire me. Keep sharing your stories with the world.

To Dean Winchester. One of the best characters EVER. Don't argue with me on this. *Supernatural* will go on FOREVER.

To Sweetie, Milkyway, KitKat, M&M, Reeses, and Twix. You saved my life. I don't remember the person I used to be before you came. Your unconditional love shows me why the world (flawed as it is) is still worth living in. I wake up with a smile on my face every day. Cat-kisses forever.

And to you, dear reader. I do hope that you enjoyed reading Nathan and Preston's journey from friendship to something more. I have always been a believer in everyone's right to love. We no longer live in a boy-meets-girl world. I'd like to believe that we are now in a person-meets-person world. So fall in love. Fall deep. Fall hard. There will be hard times. There will be happy times. But never close yourself to the possibility of love.

Turn the page for some

Sw♥♥nworthy

Extras....

Nathan's European Adventure Itinerary for Lovers

Planning your own European adventure? Bringing someone you love with you? Nathan suggests that you try to visit these places. Take lots of pictures. Declare your undying love. Hopefully the universe is on your side and it won't take ingesting a magic pot brownie to confess. *winks*

I know it looks like a hectic few days, but Nathan knows his stuff. I suggest marking all these places down and making your way through Europe the way Nathan and Preston did. I also suggest bringing your copy of *No Holding Back* with you and snapping pics with it. Send them to me if you do! Just tag @KateEvangelista and @SwoonReads on Facebook, Twitter, or Instagram.

Paris, France

DAY 1

In the morning
Luxembourg Gardens (visit duration: 2 hours)
Pont des Arts* (visit duration: 15 minutes)
Royal Palace (visit duration: 1 hour 30 minutes)

In the afternoon
Sacré-Coeur Basilica (visit duration: 1 hour 30 minutes)
Place du Tertre (visit duration: 1 hour 30 minutes)

SwoonReads

DAY 2

In the morning

Musée d'Orsay (visit duration: 2 hours)

Hôtel des Invalides (visit duration: 1 hour)

Rodin Museum** (visit duration: 1 hour 30 minutes)

In the afternoon

Eiffel Tower (visit duration: 2 hours)

River Cruise (visit duration: 1 hour)

Arc de Triomphe (visit duration: 1 hour)

DAY 3

In the morning

Pantheon (visit duration: 1 hour)

Notre-Dame (visit duration: 1 hour 25 minutes)

Holy Chapel (visit duration: 1 hour)

In the afternoon

Louvre Museum*** (visit duration: 2 hours)

Palais Garnier Opera House (visit duration: 1 hour)

Tuileries Gardens (visit duration: 1 hour)

Traveler's Notes:

*Visit the Pont des Arts for the love locks. In the book, it is mentioned that they have been removed. If they are still there when you visit, please take a moment to bask in all the love attached to those locks. If they are no longer there, please have a moment of silence for the lack of locks.

**For every art museum you visit, think of Didi. I know she doesn't make much of an appearance in this book, but that's what Nathan and Preston did.

***Try not to criticize the *Mona Lisa* too much. Wouldn't want to make a tourist cry.

Swoon Reads

Cork, Ireland

DAY 1

Blarney Castle* (in the morning)

The English Market** (in the afternoon)

DAY 2

The Beara Peninsula (all day)

DAY 3

Fota Wildlife Park (in the morning)

Old Midleton Distillery (in the afternoon)

Traveler's Notes:

*The Blarney Castle is huge, so really take all morning to explore its nooks and crannies. Plus, you can't pass up the chance to kiss the Blarney Stone. Grab that gift of gab for yourself.

**I say eat your way through the English Market.

Rome, Italy

DAY 1

St. Peter's Basilica (in the morning)

Trastevere District (in the afternoon)

DAY 2

In the morning

Santa Maria della Vittoria (visit duration: 1 hour)

Santa Maria degli Angeli (visit duration: 1 hour)

Palazzo Massimo alle Terme (visit duration: 1 hour)

San Pietro in Vincoli (visit duration: 2 hours)

In the afternoon

Via dei Fori Imperiali (visit duration: 1 hour)

Colosseum (visit duration: 1 hour)

Basilica of San Clemente (visit duration: 1 hour)

DAY 3

Casa di Giulietta* (all day)

Traveler's Notes:

*If Nathan hadn't gotten sick, he definitely would have taken Preston to Juliet's House in Verona. It's just a short trip out of Rome by train. Fact: Nathan's favorite play is Shakespeare's *Romeo and Juliet*.

Santorini, Greece

DAY 1

Agios Georgios* (all day)

DAY 2

In the morning

Pyrgos Village (visit duration: 45 minutes)

Monastery of Profitis Ilias (visit duration: 1 hour)

Megalochori Village (visit duration: 2 hours)

In the afternoon

Vlychada Village (visit duration: 2 hours)

Akrotiri

DAY 3
Day cruise to:
Nea Kameni
Palea Kameni
Thirassia Village

Traveler's Notes:

*In the book, Preston and Nathan spend the entire day at the beach. Natasha ends up kidnapping them to Amsterdam. But if you want to keep with the three-day-tour stay that Nathan initially planned out, then stick to his original itinerary.

Amsterdam, the Netherlands

DAY 1
In the morning
Rijksmuseum (visit duration: 2 hours)
Vondelpark (visit duration: 2 hours)

In the afternoon
Van Gogh Museum (visit duration: 2 hours)
Amsterdam Canal Cruise (duration: 2–3 hours)
Paradiso*

DAY 2
In the morning
Begijnhof (visit duration: 1 hour)
Flower Market (visit duration: 1 hour)
Anne Frank House** (visit duration: 2 hours)

In the afternoon
The Jordaan (visit duration: 2 hours)
Red Light District

DAY 3
In the morning
De Oude Kerk (visit duration: 2 hours)
Royal Palace Amsterdam (visit duration: 2 hours)

In the afternoon
Leiden Square*** (Leidseplein) (visit duration: 2 hours)
Albert Cuyp Market (visit duration: 2 hours)
Heineken Experience (visit duration: 2 hours)
Royal Concertgebouw (visit duration: 2 hours)

Traveler's Notes:

*Paradiso is an awesome club. Make sure to take in a show and dance the night away. Preston and Nathan sure did. A pot brownie may have been involved.

**If you've read *The Fault in Our Stars*, then this is a place you cannot miss!

***Amsterdam is known for awesome street food. I say eat your way through the city as well. Try their döner kebabs, croquettes, french fries with mayonnaise, and the Automats. The food is seriously good.

Venice, Italy

DAY 1
In the morning
Doge's Palace (visit duration: 2 hours)

Caffè Florian (visit duration: 1 hour)

In the afternoon
St. Mary of Health Basilica* (visit duration: 1 hour)
Ca' Rezzonico (visit duration: 2 hours)
Campo del Ghetto (visit duration: 2 hours)
Paradiso Perduto (visit duration: 2 hours)

DAY 2
In the morning
Gallerie dell'Accademia (visit duration: 2 hours)
Ca' d'Oro (visit duration: 2 hours)

In the afternoon
Ca' d'Oro alla Vedova (visit duration: 2 hours)
Arsenale di Venezia (visit duration: 3 hours)

DAY 3
In the morning
Venetian Lagoon (visit duration: 3 hours)

In the afternoon
Duomo di Murano Santi Maria e Donato (visit duration: 2 hours)
Gondola Ride** (duration: 1 hour)
Locanda Cipriani (visit duration: 2 hours)
Rialto Bridge*** (visit duration: 2 hours)
Caffè del Doge**** (visit duration: 1 hour)

Traveler's Notes:

*Preston and Nathan take one of their sweetest pictures here, where Preston realizes he and Nathan will be together forever.

**Preston took Nathan on a gondola ride in the hopes of it being romantic. It sort of wasn't for them, but definitely try it when you're in Venice.

***Go shopping at the Rialto Bridge and take lots of pictures.

****Don't leave Venice without having coffee at Caffè del Doge. Their brew is to die for.

Preston's Chicken Noodle Soup of Love Recipe

Someone you love feeling under the weather? Well, take Preston's lead and make some chicken noodle soup. This recipe will serve three to four when you're done, so make sure to keep the rest in a plastic container for reheating. You'll have your loved one feeling better in no time!

INGREDIENTS:

1 tablespoon butter

1/2 cup chopped onion

1/2 cup chopped celery

4 (14.5 ounce) cans chicken broth*

1 (14.5 ounce) can vegetable broth*

1/2 pound chicken breast (cooked and chopped)

1 1/2 cups egg noodles**

1 cup sliced carrots

1/2 teaspoon dried basil

1/2 teaspoon dried oregano

Salt and pepper to taste

DIRECTIONS:

1. In a large pot over medium heat, melt butter.
2. Cook onion and celery in butter until just tender, five minutes.
3. Pour in chicken and vegetable broths and stir in chicken, noodles, carrots, basil, oregano, salt, and pepper.

Swoon Reads

4. Bring to a boil, then reduce heat and simmer twenty minutes before serving.

Simple as four steps. I say if you know how to boil water, you can make this soup. Plus, at the end of the day, it's the thought that counts. So, make your loved one swoon by taking care of him or her while he or she is under the weather.

Note:

*Preston makes his broth from scratch. You don't have to if you're in a pinch. Broth takes hours to make. The canned stuff is good too. Just be careful not to add too much salt, since canned broth tends to already be salty. As Preston says, "Season to taste."

**For the noodles, Preston prefers the freshly made kind. But if you don't have access to those (and those tend to cook faster), the dried kind works too.

A Coffee Date

with author Kate Evangelista and her editor, Holly West

Getting to Know You (A Little More)

Holly West (HW): What book is on your nightstand now?
Kate Evangelista (KE): I just finished *Simon vs. the Homo Sapiens Agenda*. So good!

HW: Good to know! That's coming up on my to-read list as well. What's your favorite word?
KE: Debauchery. Four syllables and naughty to the highest degree. (Is that bad? *giggles*)

HW: Nah. You have to love a little bit of debauchery. In the right setting, of course. ;-) And speaking of settings . . . If you could travel in time, where would you go and what would you do?
KE: Victorian England, because of the dresses. I always love myself in a corset. And I would stroll around Hyde Park in the afternoon.

HW: Do you have any strange or funny habits? Did you when you were a kid?
KE: I don't know if you can call it strange, but I would always find myself in someone else's house as a kid. Every afternoon I would sneak out of my house and walk around our neighborhood, knocking on doors, and somehow (I don't know how) people would let me in and feed me. I guess you can say I'm like a cat that way.

HW: Nathan and Preston travel to several different European countries. Have you ever been to Europe yourself? Any fun travel stories to share?

Swoon Reads

KE: Confession: I have never been to Europe. *gasp* But the stories my parents told me were so vivid, it was almost like I was there. It's on my bucket list. As for funny travel stories, I was once stopped by a beagle (basically Snoopy) at immigration as I was entering the US. I took a ham sandwich with me from the plane that I didn't eat. Apparently airport security frowns upon that. I honestly thought they were going to deport me. *cries* They had all my bags checked because of it. And I only had a thirty-minute window between then and my connecting flight! The plane was already boarding when I got to the gate. Nerve-racking at the time. Hilarious now. Suffice it to say, I learned my lesson. Never bring food down from a plane.

The Swoon Reads Experience (Continues!)

HW: What's your favorite thing about being a Swoon Reads author so far?
KE: Everything. I sincerely believe I have found my home. Please don't make me leave. (Again, I'm a cat that way.)

HW: How has the Swoon Reads community impacted your experiences as an author?
KE: The support was overwhelming. This was during a dark time in my writing career. When I thought I was no good as an author. I guess you can say the Swoon Reads community put me back together and helped me heal.

HW: Did *No Love Allowed* being chosen change your life?
KE: In the best way possible. I get to work with awesome people. I get to write the stories I love. And I am honored to be a part of the best group of authors on the face of the planet. So yes: Life changed!

HW: Do you have any advice for aspiring authors on the site?
KE: Edit. Edit. Edit. Just because you weren't chosen the first time,

Swoon Reads

take a moment to reread your story, edit, and resubmit. Not being chosen the first time isn't the end of the world.

The Writing Life

HW: Where did you get the inspiration for *No Holding Back*?
KE: I've always wanted to write an M/M romance. Because of *No Love Allowed*, I was introduced to Nathan and Preston. They were kind enough to let me share their story with the world.

HW: Second books are notoriously difficult. What was the hardest part about writing *No Holding Back*?
KE: Getting Preston's voice right. He was such a quiet force in *No Love Allowed* that I couldn't hear him properly as I was writing *No Holding Back*. Nathan, in all his fabulousness, was drowning him out. But I think, after several drafts, we finally got our cussing swimming god to open up. *laughs*

HW: What's your process? Are you an outliner or do you just start at the beginning and make it up as you go?
KE: I used to start at the beginning and let the characters speak to me, but now that I'm writing straight-up romance, I find that it helps to lay out everything. Not the plot, per se. I still leave that up to what the characters tell me about their story. What I mean is I have a corkboard with multicolored index cards that show me the name of the character, what they look like, what their flaws are, what tropes I plan to use in the story. Little things that keep me on track as I write.

HW: What do you want readers to remember about your books?
KE: That everyone deserves to be loved.

No Holding Back

Discussion Questions

1. The book is dedicated to love and how it is too beautiful to hide in a closet. What does "too beautiful to hide in a closet" mean for you? How is the book connected to this inscription?

2. Nathan dreams of becoming a party planner at an early age. What were your dreams at the age of thirteen, and how have they changed now that you have gotten older? What dream are you working on fulfilling?

3. Preston is devoted to swimming. He eats, sleeps, and breathes it. Do you know anyone in your life with the same single-minded commitment to a goal? Has there been a time in your life when you've obsessed about wanting to get something or get into somewhere?

4. Do you agree with how Nathan handled Preston's need to obsess? Why or why not? Would you have gone as far as taking his phone away?

5. Nathan is a romantic, as evidenced by his love for *Pretty Woman* and his plans for romantic confessions. Do you see yourself as a romantic? Has there ever been a time when you planned on telling someone you loved them? How did that go?

6. As the book progresses, we see Preston realize there is more to life than practice. Can you relate to how he was feeling? Or if not, why?

7. Natasha believes that Nathan is overthinking things—that he should have just come out and told Preston how he felt from the beginning. What would you have done in Nathan's situation?

8. After Nathan's confession, Preston seems not to address these feelings in favor of taking over the last leg of the trip. Put yourself in Preston's shoes. Would you have come out with your own feelings during breakfast the day after or would you have kept things a secret so you could plan your own perfect confession?

9. When Preston finds out he got into the Bennett Club, he completely forgets about the date he had planned with Nathan. What did you feel in this moment? Should Nathan have reminded him of the date? Was he right to let Preston go?

10. Do you think *No Holding Back* is an issue book (a book that addresses a particular situation/problem in readers' lives)? Why or why not? What are your thoughts on the author's treatment of Nathan and Preston's road to love?

Swoon Reads

What better way to get over a breakup
than to set up your best friend?

Why focus on your own problems when your
friend's love life is so much easier to fix?

Meg
&
Linus

HANNA NOWINSKI

COMING SOON

Meg and Linus, two best friends bound by a shared love of
school, a coffee obsession, and being queer, must break out
of their comfort zones and learn how to stand on their
own in this fun debut novel by Hanna Nowinski.

I quickly look back at my lunch tray as soon as I realize what I've been doing, but it's too late—Meg has already turned her head to see what captured my attention, and when she looks back at me, there's this little gleam in her eyes that rarely means anything good.

To make matters worse, I can feel myself blushing quite furiously.

"I see," she says, sounding very smug about it.

"No, you don't," I try, but she just smirks widely.

"He's cute."

"I really hadn't noticed."

The way she is able to raise one eyebrow almost to her hairline has always been slightly frightening to me, and it's even worse when that look is directed at me.

"Meg—" I start, but she interrupts me.

"Can it. He's joining drama club, and you know it, don't you? Your secret plot has been revealed."

"There is no secret," I assure her. "Please, just let it go?"

"No, we should totally join the drama club," she says. "Trying new things is good. And it would give you the perfect excuse to talk to him."

That makes me laugh. "Like he'd be interested in talking to me."

She frowns at me. "What's that supposed to mean?"

I shrug. "I'm kind of chubby and a bit boring and he is, like, really good-looking and probably has a million friends—"

"Okay, what does his number of friends have to do with anything?" she asks, confused. "And he's a drama geek; they're not exactly popular, either, are they?"

"He's more popular than we are."

"Sophia was in drama club," Meg reminds me. "And she still dated me. For two years."

"All right, but—"

"Also, you're cute as a button," she continues. "He'd be lucky to have you!"

"I'm not—"

"And since when are you boring? When have you ever been boring?"

"My idea of a perfect Friday night is rewatching *Firefly* and then reading until I fall asleep on the couch."

"So?"

"I own not only a pair of *Star Trek* pajamas but also Batman pajamas."

"Which are both awesome."

"The Batman pajamas have a cape attached to them."

"Even more awesome!"

"I actually *like* going to class."

She groans and throws both hands up in frustration. "Because you actually like most things! You're one of the most passionate and intelligent people I have ever met in my life—how is that a bad thing?"

I stare sullenly at my pasta that's slowly getting cold and scowl just to prove her wrong, even if all the nice things she is saying about me just make me want to get up and hug her. "Meg, can you honestly see someone like him even looking at someone like me?"

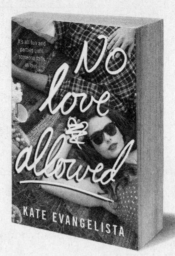

When **KATE EVANGELISTA** was told she had a knack for writing stories, she did the next best thing: entered medical school. After realizing she wasn't going to be the next Doogie Howser, M.D., Kate wandered into the literature department and never looked back. Today, she is a graduate of De La Salle University–Manila with a bachelor of arts in literature. She taught high school English for three years and was an essay consultant for two. She now writes full-time and is based in the Philippines.

kateevangelista.com